Mating Season

Also by Alice Gaines

Mating Season

A Cabin Fever Novella

ALICE GAINES

AVON

Excerpt from *Heat Rises* copyright © 2012 by Alice Brilmayer.
Excerpt from *Night of Fire* copyright © 2012 by Nico Rosso.
Excerpt from *Storm Bound* copyright © 2012 by Alice Brilmayer.
Excerpt from *The Short and Fascinating Tale of Angelina Whitcombe* copyright © 2012 by Sabrina Darby.

EPub Edition AUGUST 2012 ISBN: 9780062210616

Print Edition ISBN: 9780062210623

10 9 8 7 6 5 4 3 2 1

Chapter One

THE FOUR-WHEEL DRIVE monstrosity came over the crest of the hill with a growl of gears and headed down the path toward the cabin, bringing Gayle Richards's worst nightmare with it. Professor Nolan Hersch didn't drive any old SUV to research sites, like normal people did. No, he had to command something hypermacho, a vehicle one might pilot out into the bush to harass lions.

The trees had stopped dripping after the recent early fall rain, but the ground remained damp, and the ferns drooped with moisture. The redwood duff, which in summer had consisted of a fine powder that coated everything that touched the ground, now made an equally fine mud. Hersch's vehicle followed the path her own tires had made until he pulled up in front of the cabin and turned off the engine.

Dressed in khakis and with his sandy hair attractively tousled, he resembled a big game hunter more than what he was—an evolutionary biologist with an ego almost as big as his reputation. She instinctively took a step backward as he climbed out. She would have wrapped her arms around her ribs, too, but he'd recognize that as a defensive gesture, so she let them hang by her sides.

He gave her his usual killer smile—perfect teeth and all—and extended his hand. "Professor Richards."

She gave him her own hand and shook firmly. Businesslike. Assertive. "Welcome, Professor Hersch."

Somehow, despite Northern California's notorious fog, his arms were tanned and covered with bleached golden hairs that set off the silver band of his heavy watch. His wrist made hers appear tiny as his hand engulfed hers. Appealing and intimidating all at once. When she'd satisfied the bounds of collegiality—and stopped staring at his skin—she pulled back.

"Good of you to have me," he said. "I enjoyed your last paper."

Oh he had, had he? Despite the fact that it blew a hole the size of his SUV through his own last journal article? Courtesy would suggest she compliment his work in return. She didn't.

He put his hands on his hips and glanced up at the cabin, which gave her a view of his Adam's apple and the gap of his shirt where he'd opened the top two buttons to reveal more tanned skin.

"Good-looking facility," he said.

"Room for four," she answered. "Where are the others, by the way?"

"There's a road washed out back a few miles. I barely

made it through," he said. "Dave and Susan should make it here in a couple of days."

"Days?" she repeated. She'd arranged for four researchers on this trip. She'd written that specifically into the grant proposal. She might need this man's collaboration on her research to win herself more visibility in her field and therefore more advancement at her university, but she sure as hell hadn't arranged a vacation for the two of them. Especially not one that involved watching large animals having sex.

Elk might not be closely related to humans, but the males had penises and they did the deed doggie style, with a lot of grunting and snorting. So no, she hadn't planned on watching animal porn alone with Nolan Hersch.

"Something wrong?" he asked.

"There's a lot of work," she said. "There's supposed to be four of us."

"It's only a few days," he said. "The mating season will last longer than that."

"I know how long mating season is," she said. "I just didn't think . . . you and I . . ."

Oh, brother. That wasn't a sentence she could finish anytime soon, if ever. She wouldn't tell him about where her mind wandered during his presentations at conferences. She wouldn't mention her delusions that every time he mentioned receptive females his gaze lingered on her. She wouldn't share the fact that every time he turned to a chalkboard she rememorized the curve of his ass.

Just because she didn't bring any of those things up didn't prevent him from watching her whenever she became uncomfortable in his presence. Like right now. There was that pleasant expression—the half smile—that did little to hide the fact that he was assessing her with as much care as he used in studying his research subjects.

She lifted her chin and smiled right back. "I guess we have enough supplies."

He gestured with his head toward his SUV. "I have more than enough for myself. We can share."

"No need. I'm well stocked. Come on inside." She turned and climbed the stairs to the cabin. Because he still had to unload his things, it would take him a while to follow, and she could catch a breath before having to allow Nolan Hersch into her space. She'd spent the last two days alternating between steeling herself for his arrival and telling herself it was no big deal.

The others were supposed to come with him. His two graduate students would have acted like a buffer, always underfoot, always between them. She wouldn't have had to imagine him alone in the next bedroom because he'd have a roommate, as would she. And when he spouted some bit of sexist bullshit from his research, she'd have support from at least one other woman. Alone, she'd end up wanting to tear him apart one way or another in an hour. Two, tops.

She went to the kitchen area of the cabin, poured herself a glass of water from the tap, and turned to lean against the counter to drink it. After a minute or two, Hersch entered with more than enough stuff for a season in the field. He needed several trips to haul it all in. Among the boxes and cases stood one of those canvas carriers wine stores sold. The necks of six bottles stuck out the top.

"A treat," he explained. "You and I can share a bottle before the others get here."

"I don't think—"

"Say, that's a fine genealogy you've done." He walked to the wall where she'd unrolled butcher paper so that she could create a visual display of the relationships among the animals they'd be observing.

He lifted a hand to trace one particular family's line. "You have three generations here."

"I've been studying these guys for years."

"So why did you invite me?" he asked.

An innocent question. A logical one. She could lie and tell him that she'd come around to his way of understanding animal sexual behavior. Or she could give him the truth . . . that he was top in the field and papers they did together had an easy shot of getting into the best and most-read journals. She wouldn't add that spending time with him in the forest was supposed to be chaperoned by the others.

"I thought it was time we collaborated," she said.

"Instead of yelling at each other at conferences?" His eyes took on the gleam of challenge she'd seen in them so many times. The blue of his irises always seemed to darken, as they did now.

"I don't yell."

He made a noise that was half humph and half snort. Maybe more than half snort.

"All right, I raise my voice," she said. "But your theory ignores the female in the mating equation."

He crossed his arms over his chest. "I promise you, I've never ignored the female."

Cute. Double entendre. His typical ploy to make his presentations "sexy." "But you do. You make it sound as if the cows stand around, grazing, while the bulls do all the work. Fighting with each other. Then she has no choice and the winner climbs on and slam-bam-thank-you-ma'am."

He laughed. "I don't think I ever put it quite like that."

"That's what you mean."

"You think I believe that?" he said. "That females have no sex drive at all?"

She glared at him, using every bit of willpower not to grind her teeth. "We're talking about animals here."

"I am. What are you talking about?"

"The way you look at things," she said. "You're completely androcentric."

One of his sandy brows quirked upward. "You think I'm fixated on the male point of view and incapable of understanding the female?"

"Something like that." Damn it all, it hadn't even taken an hour for him to get under her skin. Not even half an hour.

"And I imagine you're going to show me how females look at things," he said.

"Animals."

"Animals," he said. "Should be interesting."

NOLAN COULDN'T HELP chuckling to himself as he sat at the long trestle table, setting up his laptop. To say that he made the woman uncomfortable was an understatement. Every time he got near to her, she either backed away or vibrated with nervous energy. He really shouldn't enjoy nettling her so much, but Professor Gayle Richards made such a delicious opponent. She didn't hang back from a debate, pretending detachment and citing references. She charged into the argument, intellectual fists flying.

The fact that her skin flushed and her dark eyes seemed to shoot sparks only added to the fun. She probably wasn't aware that her lips pursed and her hair—curls the color of dark chocolate—fell into her face as she lit into his ideas. This afternoon, Nolan would have tucked her hair behind her ear for her, but that would most likely have gotten his hand slapped. So he'd stood there smiling in the way he knew would most irk her and enjoyed the view.

Finally, she'd huffed and stalked off to disappear inside her room. Before she'd left, he'd gotten another view of the fun side of her. A truly voluptuous figure hidden inside worn blue jeans and a T-shirt from her university. She obviously had no idea what the faded denim did for her hips and butt or how it made her legs seem to go on forever. And if she'd wanted to hide the swell of her breasts, she should have bought a larger shirt.

Intellect, body, and the most kissable mouth this side of the Continental Divide. He hadn't lied when he'd told her it was going to be an interesting few days.

He was probably invading her space more than necessary by putting his computer right next to hers, where they'd share body heat if they tried to get some work done together. They had quite a history, although they'd never worked together. They sparred in scientific papers, and every time they ended up in the same room they forged a physical connection. Sometimes arguing, sometimes avoiding each other, but each of them always knew where the other was. Just as he now felt her every movement in his bones as she moved around the corner of the room that served as a kitchen.

Something smelled really good back there, and he'd sneaked a look long enough to see her put a large pot of water on the stove to boil. Dinner would be pasta of some kind, and if he could think up a good one-liner, he'd needle her about her domestic skills.

She thought he was a sexist creep, although she never used those words. Instead, she referred to him with jargon like *androcentric* or *masculinity-obsessed*. Silly, politically correct arguments did no justice to her otherwise excellent intellect, but they made great ammunition for the sort of heated debates he most enjoyed. Alone here for several days, he could yank her chain and enjoy the sparring to his heart's content. So he would.

Smiling to himself, he searched through the file of videos on his laptop until he found the one he wanted. After turning up the speaker, he clicked the play button. An image of a full-grown elk with impressive antlers appeared. After a few seconds with no sounds but bird calls, the male threw back his head and bugled loudly enough to echo off the trees.

Back in the kitchen, something crashed, and Gayle muttered, "Shit."

Nolan had to stifle a chuckle. He turned to find her bent over the remains of her coffee mug. A brown stain was crawling over the wooden floor.

"Did I startle you?" he asked as innocently as he could manage.

"Yes." She straightened. "That is, no."

"You're sure?"

"I dropped my coffee," she answered as if that explained everything.

"It's just the elk's mating call."

"I know what it is. I've heard it often enough." She tossed the pieces of her mug into the trash and got a few paper towels from the dispenser.

"Magnificent, isn't it?" He turned back to his computer and played the video over, nudging the volume up a bit. "The male in full rut. This bad boy must have quite a harem."

"I'm sure." Sarcasm dripped from her voice. If she didn't approve of harems, she should have studied another animal. She could have gone into psychology, where she could show people ink blots or make up questionnaires. She was far too good a scientist to deal in anything but facts, though, even if they contradicted her view of how the world ought to be.

"Have you seen one this big?" he asked.

Her head snapped around, and her eyes went round.

"The bull," he said. "Have you seen one this big?"

Her shoulders almost—not completely—sunk back to where they belonged. "Why are men so hung up on size?"

"Sexual selection probably. To attract mates."

"Oh brother."

"You think size has nothing to do with a male's appeal as a mate?" he asked.

"I think I'm going to grate some cheese." With that, she opened the refrigerator and stared inside. When she bent to look on one of the lower shelves, she gave him a great view of her backside. A perfect upside-down valentine—slender at the waist and flaring into every ass man's wet dream, including his.

Pretending to ignore him, she pulled out a hunk of what looked like the really good Parmesan, took it to the cutting board, and proceeded to pass it along the fine side of a square grater.

"You do that yourself?" he asked.

"It tastes better than the stuff in the box."

"All the comforts of home." He put his hands behind his head and leaned back in his chair. "I should have brought a woman along on one of these trips long ago."

There went the flash of anger in her eyes. "I brought you along. This is my grant, remember?"

"You're right. My apologies." Of course he knew that. He hadn't forgotten for an instant. Her name would appear first on any articles they might produce. He wasn't the Neanderthal she thought he was, but he also wasn't above playing one if it got a reaction from her.

"Besides, you've taken women on field assignments before," she said.

"You noticed."

"Well sure . . . everyone knows . . . I mean . . ." She sputtered to a stop.

"Like Susan," he supplied.

"Exactly. Like Susan," she said.

"But as you said, I've had female colleagues before now." Actually, he sponsored more women for degrees in the field than most men and even some women professors. He took his female colleagues as seriously as he did the male, and it would frankly irk him that this particular female didn't believe it except for the fact that he had so much fun irking her in return.

"It isn't any of my business," she said. "Why don't you open a bottle of that wine?"

"Good idea."

The sun had set a while before, and darkness closed in quickly under the towering redwoods. Because power came from a generator, only a few small lamps illuminated the room. They might as well be having a candlelight dinner. Romantic. A scene for seduction, if he'd planned any such thing. Of course he hadn't. Just a little bit of wordplay to pass the time.

Although they worked at different universities, they were still too close in an insular field to have an affair. Tongues would wag. Anything one of them said about the other's work would be attributed to their sexual relationship, not honest evaluation. No he'd have to keep the mental pictures of having her ride his cock to his fantasies, where they belonged. Damn it all to hell.

By the time he'd found his corkscrew, sorted through the red wines to select a zinfandel, and poured two glasses, she had the rest of dinner on the table. Small dishes of green salad stood on either side of a platter of spaghetti topped with thick tomato sauce, with chunks of sausage and meatballs. The perfume of garlic and basil floated all around them.

"Sorry I didn't bring a baguette," he said as he handed her a glass and took his seat.

"You didn't know the menu," she said. "Enjoy. We'll be eating out of cans before we leave."

"Dave and Susan will be here in a couple of days. I'll call and tell them to bring more wine."

"Can't." She lifted her glass in a toast. "No cell towers out here."

He clinked his glass against hers. "We really are isolated."

"So it would seem." In the dim light, her eyes seemed fixed on his face, her gaze full of interest or curiosity. There was the connection he'd felt before. More than once, he'd glanced across a reception or a lecture hall to find her staring, only to look away when he caught her at it. That's what had told him she never lost touch of him any more than he did of her.

Finally, she took a sip of her wine. "Wow."

"The good stuff. " He held up the bottle so she could read the label. "Rosenblum."

"Rockpile Vineyard, the *really* good stuff."

"So's the food." He put a heap of pasta on the plate in front of him, added a meatball and some sausage, and passed it to her. Then he took her dish and served himself.

They ate in silence for a while—not the companionable silence of people who've talked long into the night and already knew each other's stories, but the sort where hands felt too large and objects moved awkwardly. They'd had this awareness for a couple of years now but had never had to spend time alone together. They'd always had colleagues around and escape routes into other rooms. Staying in this cabin together, they'd confront each other wherever they turned. Sharing a bathroom, scheduling showers—the intimate things lovers did but with nothing resolved between them.

The discomfort even got to him, and he kept his eyes more or less fixed on his food. They took turns keeping each other's wineglasses full. Finally, though, he'd stuffed himself. He didn't have the meal as a diversion any longer.

"That was delicious," he said around his last bite of meatball. "I didn't know you were Italian."

"My mother is."

"Traditional family upbringing. I should have guessed," he said.

She put down her fork and stared at him. "Why do you assume that?"

"Because children thrive in two-parent families. They go on to achieve, as you have."

"What if she's a single mother?" she said. "Would that disqualify me somehow?"

"Is she?"

"No," she answered.

"What does she do for a living?" he asked.

"She had six kids. That's enough, don't you think?"

"And your father?"

She rested back in her chair and crossed her arms over her chest. "He's a doctor."

"What about your brothers and sisters?"

"Is there a point to this?" she asked.

"Just answer."

"Two still in college, two engineers, and a biochemist."

"And you," he said. "I rest my case."

She grabbed the wine bottle and refilled her glass. "And just what do you think you've proved?"

She knew damned well. They'd been having this battle in the journals and at symposia. He'd thought that they could get through a good meal before they'd have to engage it all over again. Maybe that was for the best. Dave and Susan didn't have to witness the fight. He poured himself some more zin and took a swallow. "The traditional family structure is the product of evolution because it works. Your own family proves that."

"Are you saying a single-parent household can't produce successful children?"

"Of course not, but the odds aren't as good," he answered. "You see the proof everywhere in the animal kingdom. The larger, stronger male protects and provides. The female nurtures the young."

"Well thank you, Father Knows Best. Are there any other words of wisdom from the 1950s you'd like to channel?"

He drank the rest of his wine and poured some more. What was left went into her glass. It turned out to be more than he'd given himself. Good. He'd need a clear head for this argument. Or at least, as clear as it could be after all he'd had to drink.

"You know I'm telling the truth," he said. "That's why you're getting so defensive."

"Defensive?" She let out a loud "ha!" "Me defensive? That's rich."

"All you've done is call me old-fashioned. You haven't cited a single piece of data to prove me wrong."

"Okay." She took a swig of her wine and thought a minute. Her eyes had the lazy look of someone who'd had a wee bit too much of the grape to be indulging in intellectual disputes. In fact, her features had softened, and a drop of wine clung to the corner of her mouth, where it would be oh so easy to lick it off.

"Lobsters," she said finally.

"Lobsters?" he repeated.

"Lobsters."

"What do lobsters have to do with anything?"

"The way they mate. The male loses interest after fertilization. The mother lobster cares for the eggs until they hatch and then spews them out by the thousands and leaves them to sink or swim." She finished her wine and sat back in her chair with a triumphant smile on her face.

"That doesn't prove anything." Damn it, his voice was rising. "They're not even mammals."

"You didn't say anything about mammals. You put forth a general theory, and I've proved it wrong."

"No you haven't."

She leaned forward and tapped her index finger against the tabletop. "Lobsters don't fit your model, and they're perfectly well adapted. We'd be up to our ankles in them if they didn't taste so good with melted butter."

"Lobsters, huh?"

"Lobsters," she said.

If he had all his mental faculties, he could no doubt find a counterargument. In the meantime, he'd made a blanket statement about evolution, and she'd found a contradicting example. All that, and she'd had more wine than he had. Relaxed as she was now, with her hair loose around her face and her features softened, she was really quite beautiful. He'd have to end the argument here and live to fight another day.

"You're cute when you've been thwarted," she said.

"Don't push your luck."

She replied with a throaty laugh, a sound that came from deep down inside her. He'd never heard that before, but now that he had, he'd never get it out of his head. The timbre of her voice was as sexy as anything he'd ever heard, the tone of a woman taking her pleasure without regard to the consequences. This situation was innocent enough, more or less. But if he followed that siren call to its logical extreme, they'd end up bed.

His cock thought that was a fabulous idea. He'd obviously had enough wine to loosen his inhibitions but not enough to dampen his ability to perform. In fact, he might have gotten them both to the perfect state of inebriation—where she'd throw caution to the winds and he could put off orgasm until he'd fucked her for a good long time, drawing climax after climax from her. And he would or die trying. She thought he was cute, huh? He'd show her cute.

"What are you thinking?" she asked.

"Nothing."

"Nuh-huh. Not true." She leaned over and tapped his temple. "There's always something going on in that high-powered brain."

He grabbed her hand. "You don't want to know."

"But I do." She bit her lip in the most provocative way imaginable, and his cock twitched in his pants. He'd wanted women before, but none of them had made him this randy. Following through was not a good idea. First, she was a colleague. Second, she would never have acted so seductively if she hadn't had so much zinfandel.

Or would she? The truth hit him right between the eyes. She might be a little loose with wine right now, or she wouldn't be taunting him so openly. But this fight didn't differ all that much from the ones they'd had in person and in print so many times before. Her eyes sparkled the same way now as they had when she'd challenged him before. She had the same passion, and that passion extended past intellect into something much more basic.

The two of them hadn't had an attraction, a mere awareness of each other. They had full-blown lust for each other. All the heat behind their earlier arguments hadn't been intellectual, but sexual. Of course, she hadn't planned this trip to seduce him, given that the others would have shared the cabin with them, but circumstances had lit the fuse, and now the dynamite was about to explode.

"C'mon, Hersch, give." She leaned closer, propping her chin on her fist. Beneath the soft material of her T-shirt, her breasts rose and fell, as if she was having trouble breathing. "I really, really want to know."

Enough. No man had to take provocation like that and not respond. He did what any male would do in that situation. He got to his feet and pulled her up after him. Something clattered to the floor, but he ignored it and smothered her mouth with his own.

In seconds, he lost himself in the kiss. Her lips were soft under his. Pliant. Giving and taking. Driving him on. She moaned softly as he continued tasting her, nipping and stroking with his tongue. They were both breathing raggedly now as arousal claimed them.

Oh yes, she wanted this. Every bit as much as he did. She melted against him, soft where he was hard. Her breasts pressed into his chest, the nipples stiffening into tight points. While she clung to his shoulders, he palmed her buttocks, massaging and pulling her against his erection.

She'd have to feel it. She'd have to know how completely she'd excited him. That didn't stop her from rubbing against him while her lips continued her assault on his reason. She'd consented. No doubt about that. She'd given her permission to carry her to her bed, strip every item of her clothing from her body, and plunge his cock so deep in her she'd never get the memory out of her head.

Hell's bells, what was he thinking? He straightened

and stepped away from her. This was Gayle Richards—
his colleague and his chief theoretical opponent. Did he
really want to make himself vulnerable by sleeping with
her? Sex always involved feelings as far as women were
concerned. Always. Did he want to include that in the
mix of their professional relationship?

"I'm sorry," he said. "That was uncalled for."

Her gaze didn't focus completely for a moment, but
then, his was probably pretty hazy, too. His heart was
still hammering, and nothing had happened to relieve
the swelling in his pants. At least she had the decency to
appear to be in the same state.

She held up a hand. "My fault. I shouldn't have goaded
you."

"The wine was my doing."

"Yeah." She managed a phony smile. "I wonder what
they put in that stuff."

"We won't have any more before the others show up."

"Sounds like a plan." She turned away from him,
and his mind finally got a semblance of control over his
body. He really wasn't going to screw this woman. Not
tonight, not ever. He hadn't quite convinced his cock, but
he'd take command of that, too, one way or another. He
hadn't masturbated much since he was a teenager, but his
hand would have to make him happy until the others got
here and the tension eased.

She bent to pick up a fork from the floor, probably
what he'd heard clatter when he'd pulled her into his
arms. Briefly, she gave him another view of her ass, so
when she straightened, he took the fork from her.

"You go on to bed," he said. "I'll clean up."

"You sure? I made a pretty big mess."

So had he, or he'd been right on the verge of doing it. He'd cleaned that up. He could wash some dishes. He most assuredly didn't need any more of her company.

"I'm sure. Let me play the enlightened man, okay?"

"Okay." She gave him a thumbs-up gesture. "Sweet of you."

"That's me . . . sweet."

"Night." With that, she went into her bedroom, taking her breasts and her ass and her moans of pleasure with her. Days until the others arrived. He was in for a hell of a ride.

Chapter Two

THE CURSED MAN and his broad shoulders took up all the room in the blind. Gayle had had it made big enough to hold two, and she'd shared the space before, with male colleagues as well as female. She'd never felt so cramped before. Every time one of them moved, shoulders bumped, hips grazed each other. She'd even gotten her feet tangled with his.

Then came the apology, followed by the other assuming fault for the contact. Then the awkward silence settled in again. If they had to wait hours for some elk to show up, she'd surely go nuts.

"Would you like some more coffee?" he asked. God, he looked good. He probably finger-combed his hair to create just the right combination of style and casualness. Instead of khakis, he'd dressed in jeans and a T-shirt that rippled over the firm planes of his chest and abdomen.

The same uniform she wore, but he made it masculine and sexy beyond belief.

She had to clear her throat before her voice would work. "Sure."

The man had become hugely domestic ever since he'd kissed her the night before. He'd cleaned up after their dinner, and she'd found the leftovers packed neatly away in the fridge. He'd made breakfast. Nothing unusual . . . just some scrambled eggs, bacon, and toast. And then he'd washed the dishes and straightened up the kitchen after that. Now he seemed determined to wait on her, hand and foot. A thermos of coffee, concern that she might not have dressed warmly enough. She ought to appreciate all the kindness. She really ought to.

Their arms butted against each other as he handed her the cup. When he poured the coffee, his fingers brushed against the side of her breast. She jumped a bit, causing the hot liquid to slosh.

"Sorry," he said.

"My fault. I zigged when I should have zagged."

"Is the coffee still hot?"

She tried a sip and did her best not to make a face. She usually took sugar. French roast unsweetened was kind of hard to take, but he drank it black, and they only had one thermos.

"It's great," she said.

"I'm glad," he said. "I wasn't sure if I used enough water."

"Perfect."

"Thanks."

Fabulous. Just fucking fabulous. She'd thrown herself at him the night before. She might have painted "take me" across her forehead. He'd responded, sort of, before he'd come to his senses and broken things off. But not before he'd given her a taste of the forbidden. Sexual excitement so potent it ought to be a controlled substance. He'd made her crave more, and if the hardness that had pressed into her belly gave any indication, he had all the equipment to give her everything she needed.

Now she had to sit here next to him—confined to a tiny space—and wonder if maybe, just maybe, he was erect right now. Shit. Clutching at the cup with a death grip, she finished the coffee in one swallow. This time, she did wince.

"Something's wrong," he said.

"No really. Everything's fine."

"You like sugar," he said. "How could I have forgotten?"

Great. He'd noticed things about her the way she had about him. They'd had a Thing between them for a long time. A Really Big Thing. He wasn't going to give in to it, and she had to hold herself back, too. Being nice to each other when all she wanted to do was to climb into his lap and demand more of those kisses wouldn't help matters. If they could go back to fighting, maybe she could get control of her libido.

Just when it seemed as if nothing would save her from the torment, a female elk appeared in the meadow. Hattie. Old Bob wouldn't be far behind.

"Get the camera ready," she said.

He turned his attention to the equipment, and the world settled into place. They'd work as a team now, concentrating on the elk. While he aimed the camera and focused it, she lifted her binoculars to her eyes. More cows stood off in the distance. Most likely the rest of Bob's harem. She'd know better when they came closer.

"Will we see the rut today, do you think?" he said.

"Possibly. If Old Bob's fought off his opponents yet."

One sandy eyebrow went up. "You've named them?"

"After members of my family, mostly on my mother's side. There are dozens of them."

"Will Old Bob make an appearance, do you think?" he asked.

"He's never far from Hattie in mating season." More cows appeared—Rosa, Angie, and a new one Gayle had never seen before. Graceful and young, this one. After that, more appeared—so many they'd have to sort out who was who from the video. A splendid harem. Bob hadn't lost his touch. Finally, he appeared behind them, his huge antlers proclaiming him a force to be reckoned with.

Beside her, Nolan's breath caught. "He's amazing."

"Be sure to get shots of all the cows," she said.

"Yeah, yeah, but . . . wow . . . look at him."

Her teeth clenched automatically. How typical of him to ignore all the females in favor of the one male. Bob was beautiful, and in fact, she took pride in his breeding success. Not that she had anything to do with it, of course, but she'd watched him since he'd first started attracting mates. With his size, he hardly had to fight to protect his harem. The other bulls took his measure and walked away without challenging him.

Bob was amazing and magnificent and all the other adjectives anyone could heap on him, but no understanding of the species could leave out his mates and how they interacted. That didn't seem to have the least effect on the man next to her. He'd zoomed in on the obvious and didn't care about anything else.

"Hey, fella, you going to get some today?" Hersch said.

"Do you mean, is he going to mate with one of his partners?" she corrected.

"Right. Whatever." His eyes glued to the camera's viewfinder, he completely ignored Gayle as well as anything else without a penis.

"Focus in on Hattie, won't you?" she said. "I want to make sure we record her behavior."

"Hattie?" he repeated. "Which one is she?"

"The cow that showed up first."

"Right." He turned slightly to capture Hattie where she stood not far from Bob, grazing as if nothing of particular interest was going on. "Hey, Hattie, want to get lucky?"

Gayle groaned inwardly. "That's my great-aunt you're talking about."

"I'm not the one who named an elk after her."

"She's an animal, for crying out loud," Gayle said. "I never thought anyone would talk dirty to her."

"That shows a distinct lack of imagination on your part."

Before she could give him a good piece of her imagination, Bob tipped back his head and let out a loud bellow. Bugling.

"See, Bob agrees with me," Hersch proclaimed. "Now cue the bow-chicka-bow music."

Even Hattie cooperated with Hersch's porn scenario. Someone who didn't know these animals might miss the subtle shift in Hattie's posture. As Bob approached, she stood her ground, signaling her willingness by presenting her rump. With a low rumble, Bob lifted his huge body on top of Hattie's and thrust into her, his haunches moving in an ancient rhythm.

"Awww-right!" Hersch said. "Nailed her."

She slapped him on the shoulder. "Do you mind?"

He lowered the camera and turned toward her. "What? Mind what?"

"This is a scientific endeavor, not a peep show," she said.

"It's a fabulous display of nature," he said. "Can't I admire it?"

"Can you act a little, well, more mature about it?"

"Look, you invited me here to observe. You showed me the finest bull I've ever seen. He just mated successfully. I'm going to get a little excited, okay?"

"Lower your voice," she said. Of course, she'd probably been yelling since somewhere back at *You want to get lucky, Hattie?* Why in hell had she ever thought she could work with this man?

"Lower your own voice," he said. "They'll hear you."

She glanced outside to find that Bob had finished and

led his group off into the redwoods. Only a few stragglers remained, and they soon disappeared, too.

"Well, that's a morning shot," she said.

Hersch lifted the camera. "We have some data in here. We might as well go back and take a look at it."

TEASING GAYLE WAS one thing, but he might have gone too far this time. Nolan hadn't said all those coarse things about the elk to upset her. The excitement of the moment really had carried him away. She might have observed the bull she called Bob cover one of his females before, but Nolan hadn't. Video didn't do a male like that justice.

Whether he'd meant to or not, he'd irritated her enough that even after dinner she could hardly sit beside him and watch what they'd recorded that morning. But as the video came to the moment in time just before the bull approached the female, Gayle clapped a hand on his shoulder.

"Pause it," she said. "Right there. Tell me what you see."

He did as she requested and studied the images on the laptop. "Am I missing something?"

"Damn straight you are. Look."

He stared at the picture some more.

"Oh, for heaven's sake," she said. "It's Hattie. Her posture. Can't you see it?"

"Not with the video paused."

"All right, start it again." She leaned closer until the scent of her soap or shampoo wafted into his nostrils. "Right there. She's shifted, her back sort of arched. Almost a lordotic posture."

"She's assumed the position?"

"I swear to God, Hersch . . ."

"Okay. I've had about enough of that for one day." Irritation went both ways. "Sit down and explain what you're talking about."

She huffed but did as he'd ordered, her arms crossed over her chest. "Hattie was signaling her willingness. Obviously."

She could be right about that. Females of most species had some way of letting the male know they were receptive. He'd never particularly noticed it in elk, but Gayle had been watching this group for a long time. She might very well know what she was talking about.

"As impressive as Bob is, he can't get anywhere without Hattie's cooperation," she said.

"That's a bit of an overstatement, don't you think?" Nolan said. "He's a lot bigger than she is."

"Bob's good, but even he can't hit a moving target."

"All right. I know where you're going next." They'd come to their constant dispute—the thing they battled about in the journals with colleagues aligned pretty much along a continuum from traditional, accepted theories of sexual behavior to what was unfortunately guided by political correctness more than anything else. She wanted to argue for the primacy of the female drive in mating against all the available evidence. If she didn't have such exceptional skills as an observer and collector of data, she'd have totally disgraced herself years ago.

He might as well make one more attempt to get her to acknowledge reality, although the expression on her face didn't offer much chance of success. Behind those deep, brown eyes, the wheels were turning, as she mentally put on her boxing gloves for another round.

"The goal of each individual is to get as much of its DNA into the next generation, right?" he said.

"Theoretically," she said. "That isn't exactly at the top of my own personal list."

"You don't plan to have children?"

"I might, but I'd want children, not little DNA receptacles," she said.

"It's the same thing."

"To you it probably is," she muttered.

"What's that supposed to mean?"

She rolled her eyes. "Never mind."

He cleared his throat. "So both male and female ought to be interested in as much sex as they could possibly have with an eye toward lots of offspring. Except for one thing."

Her foot began to move, an angry tap of the heel against the floor. "I know what's coming next."

"After copulation, the female is stuck with the egg and then the embryo, the fetus, and the calf. She can't conceive again for a long time. Her best evolutionary bet is to keep the powerful male around to provide."

"So the male wants sex while the female wants a meal ticket, is that it?"

"You're oversimplifying, but yes."

"There's at least one little problem with your theory."

She gave him a smile the cat might give a cornered mouse. "If the male is such a hypersexual creature and the female is nothing more than a brood sow, why is it that a woman can have two, three, or more orgasms to a man's one?"

Good Lord, they'd never discussed anything like *that* in any of the journals. Could she have been thinking it the entire time? Could she have been looking at him and pondering orgasms? With his brain nearly empty of responses, he glommed onto something a professor had said to him ages ago.

"As lovely as the female orgasm is, there's no evolutionary necessity for it." Most likely, even the man who'd told him that didn't really believe it. There were lots of reasons for women to have orgasms, evolution be damned. But he wasn't going to bring any of them up with the memory of their kiss still hot in his mind.

"Oh really?" She stood, rested her hands on the arms of his chair, and leaned into him until her nose almost touched his. "How about getting her to hold still?"

"Are we back to that?" he said.

"We never left it. Look, pal." She waved a finger under his nose. "The male can bray, bugle, or pound his chest all he likes. If the lady isn't interested, he's SOL."

"So you've said. Numerous times."

"So says nature. If you observed . . . really observed . . . with your eyes instead of your preconceived notions, you'd see that's how it works in nature. No matter how big and fierce the animal, he's not getting laid until she's damned good and ready." She straightened, staring daggers at him the whole time. "When it comes to sex, the female rules."

"You've missed the point entirely." He didn't add "again," although he certainly could have.

"Oh really? " She backed away a bit, but only to get enough room to pace back and forth in front of him.

"You study elk, for crissake. You know how those animals behave. Each of the cows only has to conceive once. Bob has to impregnate them all. He'll go at it day and night while the females stand around grazing."

"So despite everything I've said, you're still going to assert that the male is more powerfully sexed than the female," she shouted.

"I'm not asserting anything. It's plain fact."

She stopped right in front of him. "Oh yeah?"

Well shit. If she could act second grade, so could he. "Yeah."

"Then prove it." She grabbed the hem of her T-shirt and yanked it up. As it went over her head, it grabbed the thing that held her hair in a pony tail, and that fell loose around her face and shoulders.

Now he found himself staring at a tiny scrap of a bra— black satin and lace—that did little to hide firm breasts just the right size for his hands. Holy shit, she'd been wearing that the whole time they'd sat in the blind together. Those long hours while he'd been killing himself to behave like a gentleman, he could have reached under her shirt and freed a nipple with only a finger. While his brain—and the smaller brain in his pants—registered that fact, her hands went to the snap of her jeans.

"What in hell are you doing?" he said.

"I'm giving you the opportunity to prove your hypothesis."

Hypothesis. Hypothesis. She was taking off her clothes, and she expected him to talk science?

She unzipped her jeans and pushed them down her legs. Only the fact that she hadn't removed her shoes and had to sit to do it now gave him a few seconds to think, or what passed as thinking as his cock came to attention. The rush of blood to his crotch came so fast and hard he might have fallen over if he hadn't been sitting down.

When she had her feet free, she stood and reached to the back fastening of her bra. "You don't look so sexual now. You look confused."

"Trust me." He swallowed hard. "I'm feeling good and sexual."

"I'm not trusting you on this one." She removed the bra to reveal the two most beautiful breasts he'd ever seen. On the small side but round, with erect nipples just begging for some loving. "You have to prove it."

"Prove it?" Damn, words were still not making any sense.

"By fucking me, of course," she said. "You can do that, can't you?"

"Of course I can."

"I was beginning to wonder after last night."

"Last night I was being a gentleman," he said.

"Gentleman." She snorted, actually snorted. "Are you male or aren't you?"

"You know damned well I am."

She removed her panties. As tiny and sinful as the bra, they hardly had enough material to make a handkerchief. When she pushed them past her ankles, she was completely, unashamedly, gloriously naked. And when she straightened again, he could let his gaze roam over all of her, from the length of her throat, to those delectable breasts, down to the flare of her hips, and finally to the heaven between her legs. All female and flushed with anger or maybe more.

"Well, are you a mindless fucking machine at the mercy of your hormones and driven by the urge to pass on your DNA or aren't you?" she demanded.

"Yes," he croaked. "Uh, no. No passing of the DNA."

Thank God he'd at least had the sense to realize that he only had one condom—the one he always carried in his wallet. With days alone in this cabin with this woman, her dirty mouth, and her body that would not quit, once wouldn't satisfy him. Once in the morning, once after lunch, and once in the middle of the night wouldn't satisfy him.

"I don't have protection," he said finally. Shit, was he really going to turn her down again? Really? Gallantry was one thing. Passing up this opportunity would amount to torture.

"You're not getting out of it that easy. I'm on the pill. So you can either prove that you can get me to hold still long enough to 'nail' me." She used air quotes around *nail*. "Or you can shut the hell up."

With the fertility problem solved, "shut the hell up" was not an option. Mindless fucking machine won. At least he had the good sense to take off his shoes before he stood to get out of his clothes. She didn't flinch when he made his intentions obvious by jerking his own shirt off. She didn't back up when he unbuckled his belt and popped the snap on his jeans. She didn't utter a peep when he lowered the zipper and pushed his pants and briefs to the floor.

She did something finally when he rose again, as naked as she was. Her gaze fastened on his erection, and she bit her lip as her eyes went wide with what looked like feminine admiration. While he hadn't had any complaints from lovers or even his ex-wife, no woman had ever looked at his member as if it was made of chocolate before.

"All right, you want to get nailed," he said. "How would you like it?"

She released a long *ahhhh*, kind of like steam escaping. "Any way you can think up."

He'd figure out the logistics later. For now, he needed that body against his own. When he reached for her, she stepped into his embrace, snuggling her curves against him everywhere. His cock nestled into the softness of her belly as his lips moved to hers for a searing kiss.

The passion of their argument immediately translated into lust delayed. Since the night before, he'd been sitting on a powder keg of thwarted need. Hard off and on all day, he'd alternated between imagining her straddling him and sinking down onto his shaft and feeling like a heel for thinking of a colleague that way. Now he could have her, and as his mouth claimed hers, he shifted so that he could finally cup her breast and feel the peak harden into a tight point.

She gasped, her lips parting to give his tongue access between them. He found her tongue as the tip probed for him, shyly at first and then with enough boldness to make his blood run hot. Whimpering, she shivered against him.

He managed to pull his mouth from hers. "Are you cold?"

"Hell no. I'm burning up."

Amazing woman. Placing his mouth at her ear, he blew a hot breath inside and enjoyed her little shimmy of pleasure. Every time she did that, she rubbed his cock with the velvet skin of her belly. Nolan wouldn't normally rush things, but if she kept doing that, she might not give him any choice. His body was an explosive, all right, and it was nearing its flash point. He'd better concentrate on her pleasure for a while to prove he could get her to hold still for him any damned time he wanted. He'd figure out the evolutionary consequences of that at some later time, when he didn't have a woman in his arms who so obviously needed the absolute best he could give her.

So after nibbling on her earlobe for a moment, he lowered his head to her shoulder and nipped the tender skin there. Delicious. Absolutely delicious. From there, her breast lay only inches away, so he laid a path of kisses to it while his hand scooped it up to savor its weight in his palm. When he flicked his thumb over the nipple, she gave him a coo of approval. The sort of sound to make his chest swell with pride and his cock to become almost painfully hard.

The urge to plunge into her grew almost overpowering, but he continued with her breast. This time, he sucked the peak into his mouth and teased it with his tongue. Her breath came hard, filling his ears with the sounds of a woman reaching her own boundary. She dug her fingers into his hair as her panting grew louder.

Had he pushed her far enough that she could take him now? Would she welcome the intrusion of his swollen member? The answer to that question lay between her legs, so he lowered his hand to her hip and then to her inner thigh. She allowed him access, even shifting to make room for his hand there. Indeed, when he stroked the lips of her pussy, his fingers came away wet.

"Don't stop," she cried.

"You want more?" He parted her petals and drove a finger inside her. That produced a stream of moisture onto his hand, so he inserted another finger and probed. She clutched at his shoulder, her nails digging into the skin. As he continued pushing and retreating, her inner muscles tensed around him. Damn, but she was hot. Ready to come in another moment. But he could do even better than that.

Instead of continuing to plunge into her, he removed his fingers and went in search of her clit. It was easy to find—hard and long at the apex of her slit. When he stroked it, she nearly fell, so he caught her with his other arm and continued pressing it and flicking against the tip.

"Oh God." She moaned. "Ohgodohgod."

Shit. He'd pushed her too hard. She was right on the

edge, and here they were standing in the middle of the living room.

"The bed," he said.

"Too far."

"Okay, but this isn't going to be gentle," he said.

"Fuck gentle."

Oh yeah, she was ready. He guided, half-carried her to the side of the room and leaned her against the wall. Crouching, he took his place between her legs and eased the head of his cock inside her. "Hang on."

"God yes." She released a sound like nothing he'd ever heard a woman make before. Low and guttural—almost a growl. Then she wrapped her arms and legs around him, and he straightened, thrusting into her in one movement.

He could have growled back or bugled like the elk in full rut. Her heat surrounded him as her muscles clamped down on his cock. She was wet, all for him. He'd created this response, drawn it from her with his hand and his mouth on her breast. So perfect, she drove him now until he felt as if he really *could* explode. With no power to hold back, he plunged into her over and over. Her back hit the wall with each thrust. She'd bruise, and he'd hate himself, but he could no sooner stop than he could sprout wings and fly out the window.

"Sorry," he gritted. "Didn't mean to hurt you."

"Hersch . . ."

"What?" *Bam, bam, bam.* Shit, was he ever going to come.

"Shut up."

He could do that. In another minute, he'd lose the

ability to speak, anyway. She was supposed to be the one on the verge of orgasm, and now he was totally going to lose control. Not fair. Why did it have to end so soon?

Just when the last thread of his sanity threatened to shred apart, her gasps turned to cries and then rose in pitch. Bless her, she was going to come first. Sure enough, her grip on him tightened, and then her muscles went wild around his cock, from the head all the way to the base. She was milking him, and he responded with a climax that started in his balls and radiated out to claim his whole body. As his shout joined hers, he released his lust into her—coming and coming until he nearly blacked out from sheer sexual overload.

He managed to hang on until it ended . . . finally. Resting his head on her shoulder, he dragged in air in gulps until he'd convinced himself that he could breathe again. She seemed to have as much trouble getting oxygen as he did, but eventually she let out a moan and a sigh. Though her orgasm had ended, her sex still grasped rhythmically around his. Proof, as if he'd needed it, that she'd come as powerfully as he had.

After a bit, she unwrapped her legs from around him and lowered her feet to the floor. Now softening and happy, his cock slipped free from her. She slumped against the wall. "Oh, my God."

"Yeah."

"That was . . ." Her voice trailed off.

"It certainly was."

She stared up at him out of dark eyes clouded with confusion. No wonder. Sex like that could scramble a brain even as sharp as hers. His own mind wasn't feeling all that clear. He'd just had a major-league orgasm with Professor Gayle Richards. Up against a wall, for the love of God.

"Are you okay?" he asked.

"Didn't I feel like I was okay?" she asked. "You were there. You must have noticed."

"I meant your back."

She lifted a shoulder and stretched. "I'll live."

"I wouldn't normally do things quite that way," he said. "Beds are a whole lot more comfortable."

"And yet, this was much more informative."

Informative? Fast and dirty, yes. Hot and sweaty, sure. Over too soon, perhaps. But what did the woman mean by informative?

"Yes." She bit her lip for a moment as the wheels turned behind her eyes. "I may have to rethink my hypothesis in light of these data."

"What in hell are you talking about?"

"My challenge, of course. For you to prove the male is the sexually superior creature."

"Didn't I just do that?" Great, he was back to shouting.

"Not at all."

"How can you say that? I just . . . and you . . . I was . . ." He gestured toward the wall as his words sputtered to a stop.

"You were consumed with lust, mindless fucking machine that you are." She crossed her arms, a perfectly ridiculous gesture that pushed her breasts up at him. "But you may have noticed that I came first."

"Of course you did. Any decent lover makes sure to satisfy his woman." Damn her, she had to realize that.

"Your woman?" Now she'd raised her voice, too. "What makes you think I'm your woman?"

He dug his fingers into his hair. "Figure of speech."

"Well, I'll leave you to figure it," she said. "We'll collect some more data tomorrow."

Nolan could only gape at her. He'd always thought her to be a sane member of the species homo sapiens. Had she been fooling him about that all this time? And what did "collect more data" mean? Was he supposed to screw her to the wall again?

"Yes, tomorrow. You'd better get some sleep." She left then. She didn't even bother to stop long enough to pick up her clothes but went straight into her room and shut the door behind her. She wasn't going to sleep with him or even invite him to sleep with her. Each of the bedrooms had two small beds. Not exactly luxurious, but one could hold two lovers if they were careful not to kick each other. She clearly didn't see him as a lover if she wouldn't share one of them, despite what they'd just done. He was a data generating machine. He ought to be offended, and as soon as he figured her out, he might be. For now, he headed to his own room. Alone.

Chapter Three

SHE'D FUCKED NOLAN HERSCH. She'd honestly gone and done it. If you got all technical about it, you might insist he'd been the one doing the fucking, pinning her to the wall like that. She'd put him up to it, though. Despite the kiss on their first night in the cabin, he'd had no intention of taking things any further. But she'd challenged him, and he'd taken her up on it. Boy howdy, had he.

Now she lay here playing the whole thing over in her mind. She'd awakened in the middle of a dream of having sex with him, only to wake up and remember it had really happened. The pleasant ache in her pussy not only served as a reminder of the fact that they'd done the nasty but also as the reaction to having taken such a large cock into her so hard and so fast. Yes, the man was endowed, and he knew how to use the thing.

She probably ought to feel ashamed of herself. After all, she didn't proposition men every day. Actually, if she thought back right to the disastrous time she'd first allowed a man to "have his way" with her, she'd never asked anyone to *shtup* her, let alone dared him to do it. Discretion was the key in academia—you didn't spread rumors, and you didn't give anyone reason to spread rumors about you. You most especially didn't order a colleague, and your main theoretical opponent at that, to prove he was a mindless fucking machine. You didn't even use phrases like "mindless fucking machine."

And yet, the glow wouldn't fade, the sensation that her skin was more alive than it had been twenty-four hours ago and that her heart beat in a stronger rhythm. That didn't make any more sense than ordering him to fuck her had, but she wasn't dealing with rationality here. He'd given her something—complete freedom to enjoy him any way she wanted. She had him all to herself for days. Days to work out her every frustration on him. Then she could simply walk away.

Whatever they'd started here would end here. He wouldn't want snickering among their colleagues any more than she did. In their small research community, rumors rebounded for years before something new came along to start tongues wagging. This was not an affair. This was a self-contained fucking and orgasm contest, and if he got any ideas, she'd set him straight ASAP. Her cabin, her grant, her rules.

She might feel guilty about that if he hadn't brought this on himself. He'd deliberately irritated her since the moment he'd arrived. He'd thought to use her anger to his advantage by getting her to stutter and stammer in the face of his impeccable logic, or what he thought was impeccable logic. Instead, his stupid male-obsessed outlook on the sex act had caught up with him. After she'd thrown down the gauntlet and he'd accepted, she really could make demands, and if he didn't meet them, he lost the argument. Either way, she won. And she might as well start collecting her winnings right now.

After tossing back the covers, she swung her legs over the side of the bed and sat up to give herself a long cat-stretch. The illuminated dial of the clock on the bedside table showed two thirty. Even a workaholic like Nolan Hersch would be asleep now. She could ambush him. If he couldn't get it up again, he'd have to admit defeat. But if he could . . . yum.

She rose, pulled her nightgown over her head to remove it, and went in search of her prey. She had to cross through the main living area of the cabin to get to his room, and she noticed out of the corner of her eye that the piles of the clothing they'd worn hours ago still lay where they'd fallen. With any luck, he slept in the nude. If he didn't, she'd get him that way quickly.

The bedroom doors didn't have locks on them, so she opened his and slipped inside. It creaked a bit, but he didn't move or make any sound except for the steady rhythm of his breathing. Sure enough, when she lifted the covers and slid in next to him, she encountered only flesh, all the way down to his butt, which was as firm and rounded as it had appeared beneath his slacks. What she didn't expect was the softness of his skin. Like velvet. Yards and yards of velvet on a body of his size.

He'd taken up the middle of the mattress, and she had to perch herself on one side to keep from falling off. With her hand on his shoulder, she burrowed her nose into the hairs at the nape of his neck. He had his own scent, kind of a combination of soap and spice with a masculine musk beneath. A prime breeding specimen, this one. When she wrapped her arm around him, he didn't stir except to issue a little snort. Still not ready to give up her explorations of his body, she held perfectly still until he settled back into sleep. Now she could let her hand wander over his chest, memorizing the curve of his muscles with her palms. She'd felt their firmness against her breasts earlier. She hadn't had a chance to circle a finger around his flat nipple, though, so she did it now.

He did exactly what she would at the caress of a nipple—exactly what she had done, in fact, with this man, several times. He tensed, no doubt experiencing a jolt of pleasure like the many he'd given her. If she continued, he wouldn't be able to stay asleep much longer, so she might as well get to the meat of things. As it were.

Skimming her hand lower, she passed the flat plane of his belly. Did he come by this body naturally, or did he have to work at it? Everything came easy for him, so he probably ate what he wanted and did what he wanted and ended up buff, anyway. She ought to hate him for that, but then, she didn't have to marry the man. She only needed to wear him out sexually.

Finally, she arrived at her destination, his cock. It wasn't completely flaccid. Hell, maybe he never got totally soft. That would explain his mistaken belief in the supremacy of the male libido. It was going to be fun to teach him a lesson or two. Or five or six or more.

As she closed her fingers around his shaft and pumped gently, his member thickened and elongated. After a few seconds, she had him well on the way to full erection. He roused a bit more and let out a low groan.

"Oh, yeah," he whispered.

"Enjoy."

"Hey." His hand closed over hers, stopping her fingers. "What are you doing?"

"That should be obvious. "She nipped his shoulder. "I'm collecting data."

"Gayle?"

"Who else?"

He rolled onto his back, nearly sending her flying over the edge of the bed. She hung on by clinging to him and throwing her leg over his. "Careful. I almost fell."

He rubbed a hand over his face. "Do you mean to say we really . . . I didn't dream that?"

"Not one second of it," she said. "You had me up against the wall like the mindless fucking machine you are."

"I wish you'd stop using that phrase," he said.

"Okay, I'll just call you my experimental subject."

He groaned again, but it didn't sound like sexual arousal this time. "You can't be serious about proving some hypothesis with me."

"Deadly serious. I'm going to shut your trap about your so-called theories once and for all."

"By fucking me morning, noon, and the middle of the night?"

"Something like that." She wrapped her fingers around his cock again. It hadn't shrunk or softened one little bit. That part of him, at least, was definitely with the program.

"And how do you plan to write up your results for the journals?" he said.

"I won't have to. Whenever you give a keynote address or read a paper somewhere, I'll be there watching you and reminding you to tell the truth," she said. "You may be an arrogant jerk, but you're not dishonest."

"Thank you," he said. "I think."

"Now, would you please lie back and let me continue the experiment?"

"I didn't agree to any of this," he said.

"You don't have to. If you refuse, then your sexual appetites aren't as strong as mine, because honestly, I've suddenly become a deranged, insatiable she-beast." She paused for a while to let the implications of what she'd said sink in. "I win."

He didn't say anything but crossed his arms over his chest. If he were fully clothed and standing in the middle of the living area, the gesture might have conveyed resolve not to surrender. The fact that he was naked in bed with an erect cock fairly pulsing against her palm kind of diluted the effect.

"Your only hope of proving I'm wrong is to try to keep up with me sexually. Come on, Hersch, give it the old college try."

"Did you run this by the Committee for the Protection of Human Subjects?" he demanded.

She sighed elaborately. "I'm through fooling around with you. If you won't cooperate willingly, I have ways to make you do it."

In one motion, she tossed back the covers to give herself room to work. Though there wasn't much light in the room—only starlight and what his own alarm clock put out—she didn't have to find his erection by feel alone. Every bit as imposing as it had seemed earlier, it jutted away from his body. With the help of her fingers, of course. Giving him no warning, she bent and closed her mouth around the tip, swirling her tongue into the pucker on the end.

"Holy shit," he said. "Damn it, Gayle, do you really have to do *that*?"

She could answer him, but that would involve using her mouth for something other than sucking on his cock, and right about now making it as hard and as big as she possibly could was more important than any verbal repartee that came to her. She had plans to climb onto this monster, plans that her own sex more than approved of. Already, moisture was collecting at the juncture of her thighs, and her clit ached to be touched and teased. Although the frantic action against the wall had stolen her breath and given her an orgasm she wouldn't soon forget, this time she'd call the shots and get exactly what she wanted.

Opening her throat, she took more of him. Not all. She could never have managed that. She sucked what she could, bobbing her head to swallow and withdraw. The rest of him she clutched in her fist. By all appearances, he was loving every minute as his fingers went into her hair and his hips rose and fell in a dance that would have only conclusion.

"You do that . . . oh, man . . . well," he said, his voice a rough whisper.

The compliment spurred her on, and she reached between his legs to feather her fingertips over his sac. He went rigid, and he sucked air into his chest with a loud hiss.

"You'd better stop. Now. Really," he said.

His tone convinced her. He wasn't messing around, and if she didn't do as he asked, the fun would end in a few seconds. She had more planned for him that a blow job. So she released him, rose to her knees, and swung a leg over him. This time, their hands met on his shaft as she held it with one hand and parted the lips of her pussy with the other.

She lowered herself onto him slowly, feeling each inch of him enter her and savoring the passage of the head deep into her. The sense of fullness from before hadn't been an illusion created by the exotic position. He really had possessed her totally, as he did right now. It was her turn to gasp in an effort to bring oxygen into her lungs. Never in her life had sex felt this good.

When he grasped her hips and set the rhythm of thrust and pullback, she matched it with a rocking motion of her own. Together, they created a complex dance of in and out, back and forth. Each slide and parry sent a jolt against her clitoris, which was now thrumming with need. Demanding more. She could come this way, but with how much more intensity with direct stimulation to that sensitive organ?

Reaching to where his sex entered hers, she dug her fingers into her curls and found her own distended flesh. When she rubbed it, she clenched her teeth to hold back an unfeminine grunt, but it escaped, anyway. So intense, so powerful. Almost too much.

His hand replaced hers, brushing her fingers aside, and he used the same maddening pressure that had driven her to the brink before. Now she didn't have to do anything but let him take control. She could simply sit astride him and let him push her and push her and push her. Placing her palms against him, she braced herself for the orgasm that would soon claim her. Oh, God, the rhythm. The heat, the hardness, the stroke of his finger against that one spot. She was going to fly apart, absolutely shatter into pieces.

When the climax finally came, it rushed through her with the force of a tidal wave. Starting at the place where Hersch kept thrusting and where his finger kept working its magic, it radiated outward to every part of her, nearly stopping her heart and squeezing every bit of air out of her lungs. She couldn't even cry out as the spasms started. His cock inside her was her anchor as her muscles kept gripping at him. For a moment, it seemed as if it would never end and that she'd die with him buried deep in her pussy. It finally did, though, and she floated down onto his chest with a whimper.

Damn it all, he wasn't supposed to be that good. A challenge among rivals wasn't supposed to turn you into helpless, hopeless mush. In a minute, she could get control of her mind again. She'd figure out where things stood and how she could regain command of the situation. It didn't help that he now cradled her in his arms and kissed the top of her head. He hadn't even climaxed, had he? One squeeze of her inner muscles and his answering gasp said he hadn't. So why was he acting so tender?

"Hersch?" she whispered.

"Hm?"

"What are you doing?"

"Letting you glow for a while," he said. "That was one hell of a climax you just had."

"Am I lighting up the room? Because I sure feel as if I could."

"Not quite. We'll have to work on that later," he said.

Later. A promise of more. She wouldn't have to fight him every step of the way. He'd given in. Game on.

While she floated on a cloud of hormone-induced bliss, he took advantage of her inability to concentrate on much of anything and flipped her onto her back. Again, she almost flopped onto the floor, but he caught her and hauled her back beneath him. Without asking for her assistance, he found his place between her legs and drove himself inside her again.

Of course. He hadn't finished. And now when he began thrusting, her body responded as it had a few minutes ago and the night before and as it likely would every time they coupled. He gazed down at her the entire time, while his cock created the most divine chaos in her pussy. Again, each stroke against her inner walls produced a friction that made her wetter and wetter. Again, he probed so deeply she could almost believe he meant to split her in two. Her clit, still so sensitive from her last orgasm, came to life, promising another climax and another for as long as he could continue.

"Not feeling quite so in charge now, are you?" he asked.

"What is it with you and talking during sex?" she answered.

"I'm on top now. Admit it."

"That's just a position. One of many possible."

"Oh yeah?" He moved harder and faster, rattling the bed with the force of his movements. She should have found it intimidating, but the total possession freed her. She had no responsibility now. She could simply lie back and take what he offered.

Or she could if her hips didn't rise up to meet his thrusts, if her hands didn't clutch at his shoulders, if she didn't taste the skin at the base of his neck. She closed her muscles around his shaft again, just to feel him shudder as he brought them both to the very edge of reality.

Just when it seemed that neither of them could take any more, he raised himself up on his fists to get a different angle of penetration. From this position, she could run her hands over his chest and watch his face. He wouldn't be engaging in any more repartee for a while.

The contortions of his face told the story of a man past his limit and well on the way to climax.

The position also brought his pelvis into greater contact with her most sensitive spot. Her vision blurred and she arched into him as the pressure built inside her, but still, she couldn't look away from him.

When his moment arrived, he threw back his head and let out a roar of triumph. Then she was climaxing with him, singing out, as the contractions hit. They came together for long seconds, the tension rippling off them and in the end, leaving them drained.

This time, he drifted down onto her, and she took his weight gladly. After all, having the air crushed out of your chest was little to have to pay after all that delicious sex. She even found the strength to stroke his back, making geometric patterns with her fingertips in the satin that was his skin.

After what seemed like minutes but was probably no more than one, he groaned and flopped onto his side. His arm hugging her ribs, he pressed his mouth to her ear. "Nice."

"Very nice," she corrected. Although the words hardly did justice to what they'd just shared.

"I hope you learned a lesson from that."

"What lesson might that be?" she asked.

He chuckled. "That when it comes to sex, the male eventually ends up in the driver's seat."

"Actually, I learned a different lesson entirely."

He didn't answer with words, but his arm tensed against her torso.

"If you didn't notice, Professor Hersch, I just had two orgasms to your one."

SHE WAS STILL in his bed when Nolan woke up in the morning. How they'd managed that without one or both of them ending up on the floor was a mystery. Well, maybe not a total mystery as she'd wrapped her arms and legs around him and he might have done a bit of wrapping himself. In any case, he unwrapped himself now. Carefully, so he didn't wake her up. As delightful as the tangle of limbs felt and as easily as his cock could stiffen in anticipation of more play, he wasn't prepared for a repeat of the brief conversation they'd had just before falling into a sated sleep. For that, he needed a few minutes to gather his thoughts, and he needed some coffee. Dark and strong and lots of it.

As silently as he could manage, he removed his robe from the hook on the back of the door, shrugged into it, and left the room. As he tugged the door quietly behind him, he listened for any sound that she'd awakened. None greeted him, so he took a deep breath and lowered his shoulders to more or less where they belonged, and went to the kitchen.

While the coffeepot gurgled away, he did his best to gather his thoughts in hopes of figuring out a way to deal with the situation. Graduate students slept with each other quite a bit, but then, they were young and unattached. Plus, the far-flung nature of what few jobs they could find when they finished made long-term relationships iffy. Once professors got to the level of tenure, they didn't usually mess around with each other. It wasn't so much because they were stodgy as because, by then, they'd usually settled down into happy marriages. He'd thought his had been happy, in any case.

This . . . well . . . thing he'd gotten himself into with Gayle Richards gnarled his gut because she'd added a whole extra layer to the sex. She was using it to make a point. They'd fought for years about their theoretical work, and now she had this to hold over his head. By her own admission, she planned to sit in his lectures and give him the evil eye if he said something she didn't approve of.

For a moment, his mind could even picture her, sitting in the back while he delivered a paper. He'd have just finished with his conclusions, and the question-and-answer session would follow. During a lull in the discussion, she'd rise from her chair—wearing something loose that buttoned up to her chin and made her look like an old-lady schoolmarm—lift her finger, and point at him. Then in an authoritative voice that carried throughout the hall she'd declare, "But on the night of such-and-such a date in that cabin in the redwoods, I had two orgasms to your one."

He groaned and leaned against the counter. She wouldn't do that, of course. No woman in her right mind would make a public declaration like that, no matter how angry he'd made her. He was going to think about it every time she was in his audience, though, and she knew it. She also knew that, no matter how arrogant a jerk he might appear to be, he'd never do anything to embarrass her.

And on top of all that . . . the *pièce de résistance*, the check and checkmate . . . he had no way of backing out of her game. Anything he did to withdraw only proved that she was right and he couldn't match her sexual demands. Even arguing that he might not *want* to match her sexual demands meant by definition that he wasn't as all-consumed by lust as she was.

The only way he could win outright would be if she suddenly decided she wasn't interested in jumping his bones any longer. She hadn't shown any inclination in that direction so far, and there wasn't likely anything in the cupboard that he could put into her coffee to dampen her enthusiasm. So his only choices were to admit defeat or to try to keep up with her.

After the last drops of coffee sizzled into the carafe, he opened an overhead cabinet and grabbed two mugs and the sugar. Great. His early-morning autopilot now included her. After setting what she'd need aside, he poured himself a cup and stood drinking it. Even the caffeine did nothing to help him figure a way out of this predicament.

The predicament appeared at the door to his room. Completely naked and curved in all the right places, she raised her arms above her head and stretched. "Great night. I slept like a log."

That was a lie, and not only did he know it but she knew that he knew it. They'd fought all night for territory in that small bed. Still, he wouldn't dignify the lie with a rebuttal, so he continued leaning against the counter and sipping his coffee.

"You made coffee," she said. "I knew there was a reason I kept you around."

"Very funny."

She approached the coffeepot, even though he stood no more than a foot away. She seemed to take absolutely no notice of the fact that she wasn't wearing any clothing, but his member noticed. In fact, it readied itself to stand up and take notice. She still carried the heat from the bed around her, combined with the scent of sex the two of them had created. Add the visuals—the slope of her breasts and the stiffness of her nipples—and she added up to the very image of a well-bedded woman.

Right now, though, she paid more attention to the coffee than she did the man who'd put out so much energy to give her those orgasms. She poured a full mug and added an obscene amount of sugar to it. After searching in a drawer for a spoon—at least he hadn't anticipated her every single need—she stirred and then took a sip.

"Not bad," she said. "I'm going to take a shower."

She turned, showing off her ass, and went into her room. Not so much as a kiss or a thanks for a job well done. She didn't even pat him on the head as she surely would have a pet dog. He'd worked his butt off to give her pleasure, and this was his reward. Utter disregard.

After a moment, she re-emerged, wearing her robe, and headed toward the bathroom.

"What if I wanted a shower?" he called after her.

She stopped. "Do you?"

"Yeah, maybe. Eventually. I wouldn't want the smell of me to drive you out of the cabin."

"That's really sweet of you, Hersch. I'll tuck that tender declaration right next to my heart."

Enough of this crap. He crossed his arms over his chest and glowered at her. "I think we know each other well enough to use first names, don't you?"

She lifted one shoulder. She wouldn't even spend the energy to give him a full shrug. "We've always known each other well enough. I prefer last names."

"Oh, that's great," he said. "It's going to make for great pillow talk, don't you think? 'Spread your legs for me, Richards. I'm going to come, Richards. I love the way you eat my cock, Richards.' "

"Did you like that?" she said. "I enjoyed doing it."

"Of course I liked it. All men like oral sex. The subject isn't fellatio. It's how we talk to each other."

"You talk the way you want, and I'll talk the way I want," she said. "In the meantime, I need a shower, and my coffee is getting cold."

He waved a hand at her. "Go on, then."

"Want to join me?" She gave him a wicked grin. "We could save some water."

"Never mind."

"Okay, you stay out here and pout. I'll just be a few minutes." With that, she went into the bathroom and closed the door.

Nolan stood staring at it for a moment. Pouting, was he? Perhaps. No one had gotten the upper hand on him since Annie had announced out of the blue that she couldn't live with only half a husband and she was leaving him to find someone who loved her more than he loved his job. Well, he'd never married this one, and he hadn't taken a vow to cherish her. He didn't have to put up with any nonsense from her, and he wasn't about to.

So he took her invitation and followed her into the bathroom, but not to shower with her—to hell with saving water. He was going to have this out.

Chapter Four

THE BATHROOM DOOR was the only one inside the cabin with a lock, but Nolan soon discovered she hadn't thrown it. Inviting him, or taunting him? Either way, he went to the toilet, put down the top, and sat on it.

The room wasn't much larger than some closets, barely holding the toilet, a tiny sink, and a bare-bones shower stall. Nothing separated him from a full view of Gayle except for a yellow plastic shower curtain with a daffodil pattern. She grabbed it as she stuck her head outside.

"Change your mind?" she said.

Her dark curls clung to her face and neck, dripping water over her shoulders. She wore no makeup, of course. Now that he thought back, he'd never seen her in makeup. She didn't need it with her clear skin and large eyes. And her mouth: that certainly didn't need enhancement. Her lips curved in the most delicious ways, especially the full lower one.

Right now, her lips were pursed as she stared at him, rather the way one studied an experiment subject. But then, that's what she considered him, wasn't it?

"We need to talk," he said.

"Really?" she said. "About what?"

"About this game you're playing."

"I'm not playing. I'm serious." She ducked back into the shower and started humming something. Whatever it was, it didn't seem to have any particular tune or rhythm. Maybe he'd finally discovered the one thing she wasn't good at—singing. As the water splashed and she continued making toneless faux-music sounds, that yellow shower curtain kept fluttering as if offering him a bouquet of plastic daffodils. Occasionally, he'd catch the outline of an elbow or a hip. One serious misstep on her part, and he'd have a complete view of her. But then, maybe she'd intended it that way.

"I'm not going to continue with your challenge," he said. "I'm a man, not an animal, and I have some choice in the matter."

"Oh, really." She stuck her head out again. "So your assertion that we ignore the primacy of our DNA at our peril no longer stands?"

"I couldn't have said anything like that."

"Hersch, Wilson, and Baumgarten, two thousand ten," she countered.

His research paper in the journal they all read. She was honestly going to stand there, naked in the shower, not six feet away from him and cite journal articles? "I didn't mean that literally."

"So, in the conclusion of your latest book, you weren't speaking literally when you said that society was organized on evolutionary principles, including different roles for men and women?" she said.

Damn, he had said that, hadn't he? It had sounded so good at the time, so profound. The book had received excellent reviews, although one or two "feminists" had objected to some of his conclusions, as if they took great pleasure in deliberately misunderstanding him. Professor Gayle Richards chief among them.

"And then, there was that reception where you declared that we were all receptacles for genetic material and the main purpose of our existence is to perpetuate the species," she said.

"That was a joke, for heaven's sake."

"A lot of people weren't laughing," she said. "A lot of people don't like to think of themselves as receptacles."

"I enjoy goading people. It makes for stimulating discussion."

"Well now I'm goading you." She whipped the shower curtain back into place, disappearing behind it—almost. "If you want to have any further discussion you're going to have to come in here."

He ought to leave. He'd taken enough from her. She could think whatever she wanted about the challenge she'd set for him. She wouldn't dare tell anyone what she'd done . . . er . . . make that what they'd done. His nightmare fantasies about her raised finger and her public accounting of orgasms aside, she couldn't exactly proclaim to the world that she'd dared a colleague to keep up with her sexually and he'd refused. She'd make herself a laughingstock.

That settled, he went to the door and even got as far as putting his hand on the knob when he realized his feet weren't going to take him away. No matter how much she irritated him, she still had a body that could get his motor running. His engine had been idling ever since she'd appeared at the door to his bedroom and stretched her arms over her head, pointing her nipples right at him. His mind might be happy asserting his dignity and free choice. His libido had other ideas.

In the end, he shrugged out of his robe, pulled aside the shower curtain, and joined her. She glanced over her shoulder to acknowledge his presence, and then tipped her head up in to the spray. She was holding the soap in her hands, working up a lather. After she put it back in its dish, she spread the bubbles over her breasts and massaged them into her skin. At the angle he was facing, he could only truly make out one breast, but that was more than enough to bring his cock to full attention. She continued, squeezing her flesh between her fingers and then tugging gently on the nipple until she'd made it into a hard, little point.

"Do you always do that when you shower?" His voice faltered on the last word, and it came out almost like a croak.

"I want to be clean."

"Then you'll want to be clean everywhere, won't you?" he asked.

She bit her lip and nodded. The perfect coquette. Who would have guessed she had that in her repertoire?

"Want me to take over?" he asked.

"Please."

Still standing behind her, he retrieved the soap from its dish and worked it between his palms until he'd filled his hands with lather. Then he ran his hand over her shoulders and down her back. He'd never thought much about that part of a woman's body being sexy, but Gayle Richards's was. Supple and graceful, with a furrow down the center. He kept making bubbles and smoothing them into her skin, even massaging her muscles with the tips of his fingers.

She sighed and stretched. "Let's exchange back rubs sometime."

"Sounds like a plan." When he got to her ass, he lathered his hands and then set the soap aside. He palmed her buttocks, savoring the curves. She was the perfect combination of firmness and softness. Sweetly rounded and only inches from his cock. When he pressed his swollen member against her, its ruddy color made a striking contrast with her pale skin.

She'd admitted to goading him, and he could always use that as her permission, or at least as an excuse. So holding one buttock in each palm, he squeezed them around his member and pumped his hips. Slick from the soap and hot water, she felt like a hot pussy as he thrust. With each move, the head of his member appeared from between her cheeks—an erotic image in its own right.

"Having fun back there?" she said.

"You know what you do to me."

"Not really," she said. "Why don't you tell me about it?"

"You make me crazy." He could hardly have thought of any better description. She drove him insane, both with her constant arguments and with the way she could send him from cool reserve to ready to cream within a matter of seconds. And if he didn't stop doing this, in another minute he'd reach the end of the line before she'd left the starting gate.

He glanced down one more time to burn the image of her butt and his member into his memory and then released her. Breathing hard, he reached over her and braced his fists against the shower wall. That brought his front flush against her back, and he could let his gaze wander over her breasts and down to her abdomen. She smelled of the soap, of course, but she had her own scent, especially her hair. Sunshine and ripe wheat. He'd noticed that about her on an unconscious level before, and now it jogged his memory. He'd always wanted this woman, from the first time he'd laid eyes on her. He just hadn't recognized the feelings until now.

She turned her head, staring into his face. Something passed between them. A recognition. There was more than a fight here, more than a clash of wills. They'd been headed in this direction since the very beginning, when he'd been a brash, young professor, full of himself after gaining tenure at a world-class university and she'd been a graduate student who'd attended one of his guest lectures. She'd stood up to him, but she'd attacked him with logic and he'd taken her seriously. They'd developed a respect for each other that day, and now that was blooming into something else entirely.

"Hersch?" she whispered.

"Turn around."

For once, she did as he asked without protest. Now he had her front, hot and slick, waiting for whatever he wanted to do, and he wanted anything and everything he could manage before his cock couldn't wait any longer and he'd have to plunge it into her. He cupped her breasts, savoring their fullness as he rubbed the nipples with his thumbs.

She moaned and reached above her to clutch the showerhead in both hands. "I swear, you're a drug."

"I hope you're addicted."

"I told you . . . insatiable she-beast," she said.

Her breasts pointed upward toward him now, the nipples begging for his caress. As he continued stimulating one with his hand, he took the other into his mouth. He'd done this before, of course, but he'd never get tired of the taste of her and how the peak stiffened even further as he sucked. He'd also never get tired of the sounds she made as she became aroused. Soft coos and sighs. So uninhibited, so hot.

He had another destination this morning, though. The ultimate kiss. He'd hear her cries as they ricocheted against the shower wall. He lowered himself slowly so that he could rain kisses down her torso and over her belly.

"Hersch, you aren't really—" she said.

"I am," he answered. "Really."

"That's no way to pass on your DNA."

"It is if it turns me the hell on," he said.

"Does it?"

"Richards, stop talking." He knelt between her legs, nudging them apart to make room for his shoulders. Now he was facing her pussy straight on. Beautiful folds and petals. All his until the others arrived, bringing the outside world with them.

He parted her lips with his fingers, and she tensed. Waiting for him to touch her, no doubt. For a moment, he'd let her savor the anticipation. The sound of her breathing filled the tiny space. When he finally stroked her from back to front, she gasped. Her clitoris was distended and ready, and when he touched it, she trembled. So responsive.

"You're doing a great job of getting me to hold still," she said.

"Odd. I thought you just shook a little."

"Maybe, but I'm not going anywhere."

"Good," he said. "Neither am I."

When he slid a finger into her pussy, her muscles squeezed down on it. An involuntary reaction, no doubt, and she'd do the same when he finally entered her. His cock fairly twitched in response. The impatient thing would have to wait for a while—as long as it took him to bring her to orgasm with his mouth.

As her moisture spilled onto his hand, he slid a second finger into her and pumped. Her hips began a little dance, the sort of automatic flex that signaled her readiness to couple. Well, she'd have to wait for that, too. Right now, he removed his fingers from her and reached behind her to pull her toward his mouth. The scent of soap mingled with the distinct perfume of her arousal. Clean, hot, and urgent, it reached inside him. He licked her slowly, stroking the inner lips and then coming back to settle on her clitoris.

As he continued caressing her slowly, the sound of her breathing rose above the pounding of water against the tiles. The combination had its own rhythm, like the lapping of waves against the shore. Droplets coursed down his face, plopping into his eyes, but he wouldn't have been anywhere else to save his life. She was becoming more and more aroused, her hips still moving so that he had to hold her against his face. She'd lose control of her response soon. Then she'd tense before the inevitable orgasm. And he would have given it to her.

Now. Her voice went higher in pitch and volume. Her body stiffened, her muscles tensing, and then she opened her throat and shouted. Though he wouldn't enjoy her convulsions this time, he continued teasing her clit until her body sagged and her knees almost gave out.

He rose quickly and caught her to pull her against his chest. She'd hung onto the showerhead the whole time. Otherwise, she would have fallen. His heart warmed with the knowledge that he could satisfy her. He'd always taken care to make sure his partners in sex enjoyed themselves as much as he did. The fact that this woman would make herself so completely vulnerable to him proved she was a braver person than he. Or maybe just more purely sensual when it came to lovemaking.

But then, hadn't that been her claim all along . . . that women were at least men's equals where sexuality was concerned? Was he going to have to rethink his position, after all? Perhaps, but he didn't have to admit it at this very moment.

"That was amazing," she whispered against his chest. "I'll never take a shower without thinking about it."

"That's going to make it pretty hard to wash your hair, don't you think?"

"It'll make it fun." She stepped to the side so that she could put her palm over his erection. "Want me to make showering memorable for you?"

"I think you just did."

Smiling, she circled her fingers around his cock and pumped him, squeezing gently at the tip on every pass. "I think we can do more than that."

He'd been hard and wanting her the whole time, and she wouldn't need to do much to make him damned fucking crazy. A few more of those squeezes would accomplish that easily. "What did you have in mind?"

"How about I grip the showerhead again and wrap my legs around your hips? You think you could manage from there?"

"I think I could happily go to my death trying."

"Give it your best shot, stud."

Stud, huh? He ought to take offense at that, and maybe he would in a few minutes, after he'd give his aching hard-on what it had needed since he'd climbed into the shower with her. He tried to raise some righteous indignation. He really did, but when she reached up and grasped the plumbing again, he lifted her legs around him. Together, they managed to maneuver into the right position for his cock to press for entrance into her pussy, and as she sank onto him, everything but the carnality of the moment flew right out of his mind.

If he'd ever been so deep inside a woman, he couldn't remember it. She surrounded him from the head of his cock to the root. Warmth everywhere, and dampness. Her body had been created for this, or his for her. She held onto him with her legs and he thrust into her. Already past the leisurely rhythm of early lovemaking, he pushed her hard and fast while the fever built in his blood.

"Nolan," she cried. "Damn, it's good."

"You know it, baby." A place in the back of his brain registered the fact that she'd used his first name and that he'd called her baby. He'd have to contemplate the meaning later because right now an orgasm was building in his balls. He couldn't stop shoving himself into her like a wild man. He was probably slamming her back into a wall again. Someday, he'd find the restraint not to do things like that. At least she seemed to be enjoying herself as much as he was.

She released a keening sound that quickly built to a shout that bounced off the walls to deafen him. She was coming, bless her, and he didn't have to hold back any longer. The orgasm took them both at the same time. Just as her pussy tensed around him, his cock released a stream of semen into her. He maintained his balance, barely, while a wave of pleasure washed through him. Her spasms drew out his response for long seconds as they hovered together in a heaven of spent lust.

When the orgasm finally ended, he did his best to catch her and pull her against him as she lowered her legs and released the showerhead.

Still after all that, remaining standing wasn't an option. Together they slid down the tiles to sit on the floor, resting their backs against the walls. The shower continued to pelt down on them as he gathered her into his arms.

"Do that often?" he asked.

"Never before," she answered. "I never imagined you'd think up doing it like that."

"I never imagined it, either," he said. "You inspire me."

"I'm glad," she said. "You were amazing."

"I amazed myself, I must admit."

She rested her head on his shoulder and moaned. "You may have something about the male being a hyper-sexual animal."

"You still had two orgasms to my one."

"I did, didn't I?"

He tucked a finger under her chin and tipped her face up to his. Her hair hung in wet curls to her face and neck, and her eyes had the soft glow of a woman thoroughly sated. No matter how insatiable she might claim to be, he could satisfy her. It bolstered his ego enough to have him strutting—if, of course, he could summon the strength to get off the floor of the shower.

"You're an incredibly sensual woman," he said.

"And you're enough man to keep me happy."

"Do you think it's possible we're both right about our theories?" he asked.

"I'll let you know when my cerebral cortex kicks back in."

Spoken like a true academic. Only a scientist would think in terms of brain geography after a coupling like that. Kind of kinky, distinctly original, and erotic as all hell. Who knew which of them had come up with the idea of having sex with the woman hanging from a showerhead? Who cared? Something about the two of them together created a magic that neither of them separately could have achieved. There was a word for that, but he wasn't going to start using it until his own forebrain had an opportunity process the possibility.

Just when that train of thought threatened to go off the rails, the shower did them both a favor by running out of hot water. At first, the temperature went to tepid, and Nolan scrambled to his feet before it became cold. He managed to turn the faucets and spare Gayle a frigid blast, but he took some in the chest for his efforts.

"Shit," he shouted as he jumped back. "Does that come out of a refrigerator?"

Behind him, Gayle giggled. "That ought to shrivel you right up."

"I try to be gallant, and this is the thanks I get."

"I bet you look like a prune." Her giggles turned to real laughter, curse her. "Are you all crinkled and tiny?"

The family jewels hung the way they usually did, but he didn't have to prove himself to her. He'd already done that several times. He wasn't her toy, despite the ridiculous game she'd tricked him into.

"Turn around so I can see," she said.

"I will not." He shoved aside the curtain and stepped out in search of what they had in the way of towels. Luckily, more than one hung from the rack, and they seemed large enough to fit around his waist. He slung one around his hips and tucked the end in, securing it twice to make sure she didn't get the satisfaction of checking him out. Then he grabbed the other towel and used it to dry his hair.

"Hey, what am I supposed to dry off with?" She'd left the shower and now stood as naked as Venus rising from the sea. She was also dripping water onto the bath mat.

"You can air-dry for all I care."

"That isn't very gentlemanly of you."

"My attempts at acting gracious don't seem to be appreciated around here," he answered.

"Well, if you're going to get testy about it—"

Before she could get even more irritating, he tossed her the towel. She caught it and rubbed the terrycloth over her shoulders and arms. Proceeding as if she shared a bathroom with a man every day, she continued over her breasts and across her ribs. It had to be a crime to treat skin like hers with so little care for its softness. If he were to dry her, he'd do it gently, licking the droplets away from the most tender places, like the curve of her throat and her nipples. Still, the way she did it created a healthy glow all over her, much like the flush that preceded her orgasm.

Beneath his own towel, his cock stirred to life. He shouldn't be able to get rigid again, and he ought to go to his room and get dressed. They had work to do, after all, and they couldn't spend the day screwing like bunnies. Or could they?

GAYLE HAD SEEN that expression on Hersch's face a few times now. He was staring at her as if she were something to eat. Come to think of it, he had eaten her a few minutes ago, and then they'd had better shower sex than ought to be possible under the laws of physics. To top that off, he'd taken a spray of cold water to the important working parts. He shouldn't be getting another boner after all that, not for hours.

Just for the hell of it, she made drying herself into a major production. She brought the towel to her breasts again, even though she'd rid herself of any dampness there. Squeezing one and then the other through the cloth, she watched his face. His gaze never wavered from her chest, and the tension of his jaw showed his concentration. She stole a quick peek at the towel that covered his pelvis. Just possibly, something was making its presence known there. Good Lord, maybe the man really was a machine.

Bending, she ran the towel over her ankles and then brought it up one of her legs to her knee then to her inner thigh. He watched that, too, color rising in his cheeks as she approached her pussy. She didn't ignore that, but rubbed it briskly, moving the cloth against the lips. Her sex had a pleasant used feeling . . . a happy ache. She certainly didn't need more sex anytime soon, but if he was offering . . . well, why not?

"Do you know what you look like?" he said.

"I have a feeling you're eager to tell me."

"Like a painting. Botticelli or one of those types."

"The women in those paintings were all fat," she said.

"Plump. There's a difference," he said. "Women should have some flesh on them."

"I had no idea you were an art critic."

"I can tell a masterpiece when I see one."

She ought to laugh at that. What an idea . . . that her body would earn such praise from a man attractive enough to entice any woman he wanted. Although it suddenly occurred to her that she'd never seen him with a lover. He'd been married, and his wife had attended conferences with him and shown up at the dinners. She'd heard via the grapevine that they'd divorced but never learned the reason why. Since then, he'd done nothing to earn himself the reputation of a player. Only his assertions that males were naturally promiscuous had suggested that he might be. Then too, he was so blessedly male, practically oozing pheromones, but maybe she'd misjudged him.

With that realization, his worshipping gaze at her body and his overblown estimation of her beauty took on new meaning. They'd forged a connection back there in the shower when what should have been casual glances caught and held. Now this. Her stomach did a flip, and she couldn't quite catch a breath. The feeling wasn't intimidating as much as it was . . . well . . . exciting.

"You're blushing," he said.

"I am?" Her skin did feel warm, and now that he'd pointed that out, the heat crept from her cheeks down her throat to her chest. "No one's ever looked at me like that."

"Then all the men you know are either blind or fools."

"I guess you're neither." She glanced pointedly at the front of his towel, which now very clearly showed a bulge beneath it. "Is that a scientific instrument, or are you happy to see me?"

"It's a scientific instrument, all right. I'm going to use it to test a hypothesis that a female colleague recently put to me."

"Then maybe that female colleague ought to make sure it's properly calibrated first."

She dropped her towel and knelt before him. Tugging the end of his towel out and letting it slide to the floor revealed that he had, indeed, become erect again. She took the shaft in one hand and gently cupped his balls with the other. "I must say, Hersch, that you do the males of your species proud."

"I am happy to see you. Very, very happy," he said.

She licked the head of his cock. "You taste like soap."

"Odd. That wasn't the last slickness all around me."

She tasted him again, this time on the underside. "Definitely soap or shampoo. It's nice."

He let out a low growl of approval. "Nice doesn't begin to describe it."

"It's great to be appreciated." She released his sac in favor of curling both her hands around his shaft. When she closed her lips over him, he took a sharp inward breath and let it out slowly. She'd felt velvet of him against her tongue before, noting the passage of the ridge against the roof of her mouth. Now she had the scent of a man clean from the shower with the undertone that belonged to this man alone. He was all sex all the time, at least for her. Now that she'd known him, other men would come up short, especially in the dimensions of their members. Still, even if she found another one as well equipped, he could scarcely rival Nolan Hersch in talent and all-around playful eagerness.

As she continued sucking on him and stroking what wouldn't fit into her mouth, he placed a hand on her head as if to maintain his balance. He was reaching the high plateau of arousal. She'd heard enough of the noises he made to know. Sighs and grunts—sounds that would seem silly in any other situation but that made a mating call to the woman who created them. They sang to her own sexual self. A serenade inviting her to the dance that would have her crooning the same melody. Her pussy grew moist, clenching in anticipation of what he'd do for her as soon as she had him ready.

She wanted him all over again. She'd had him twice the night before, in coupling so fierce it made all her other encounters seem trifling. She'd had him again just a few minutes ago, and he'd made her come so hard she'd burst into sparkling pieces. Now she needed more because he needed more. They'd satisfy each other again, but for how long? How much time would pass before the same hunger returned to demand more and more and more?

Then he was trembling and pushing her head away. "Damn, but you give good head."

"I'm only giving as good as I got."

"In another minute . . . wow." He took an uncertain breath. "Bedroom?"

"Too far.

"You always say that," he said.

"It's always true." Instead of rising, she knelt on the bath mat, offering him a view of her ass. "Why don't you mount me here?"

"Doggie style."

"If it's good enough for the elk . . ."

"I might just bugle." He lowered himself to his knees and took his position between her legs. Then grasping her hips to brace her, he eased the tip of his cock between her folds. She almost melted on the spot. He felt so fucking good. She did turn liquid, releasing moisture to coat him and invite him deeper.

He took his time about it, burning the impression of every inch of him into her mind. By the time he'd entered her fully, her heart had sped to a thready rhythm, and her clitoris had hardened and begun to throb. He truly would turn her into an addict if he kept performing like this, but for now, she wouldn't worry about the future but would enjoy his total possession of her body.

He began thrusting with a slow and steady rhythm, pulling nearly out of her and then pressing forward again. Each time he entered her, he seemed to go deeper, as if they hadn't already known each other as intimately as two lovers could. Her breathing caught the tempo, and her heart beat in double time.

"I don't believe I'm doing this," he said. "Again."

"I do believe I'll kill you if you stop."

"Stop?" He moaned in a particularly low and evil manner. "Not possible."

She'd feel flattered if she weren't so completely turned on. She might even feel feminine pride, if the higher centers of consciousness hadn't blinked out about the time he'd entered her. She'd have to figure all that out later, because she was about to hit the wall called orgasm and get splattered right against it.

"Nolan," she cried.

"I know, babe." Then he did the absolutely most fantastic thing she could have imagined. He reached around her to find her clit. As soon as he touched it, she went ballistic. Every muscle in her body tensed as the climax rushed through her. She shot straight up to heaven, shouting as her pussy clamped down on his hardness over and over. When he came, too, grasping her hips and pounding into her a few more times, he prolonged the heaven. When it ended, her strength gave out and she collapsed onto the floor, struggling for breath.

"You know what, Hersch?" she said when her voice returned.

"Nolan," he said, his mouth at her ear. He'd fallen on top of her.

"Whatever."

"Not whatever. Nolan."

"Okay, Nolan. I think you won that one."

NOLAN SHOULDN'T WEAR her acknowledgement as a badge. He shouldn't have to stifle a grin as he walked beside her along the path underneath the huge trees. He couldn't help but enjoy the day, of course. The air held a bit of a chill as it always did in the forest. So little light penetrated to the ground that even on the hottest days, the air always felt cool under the redwoods.

Few plants could grow with so little sun to nurture them, which created the effect of being in a cathedral rather than a space created by nature. Where grasses clogged the landscape in other places in Northern California, only ferns appeared here. With the tall trunks of the trees reaching toward heaven and the soft duff beneath their feet to muffle their steps, he couldn't avoid the comparison to a place of worship. This space was that beautiful.

Gayle must have shared his awe because she hadn't issued so much as one clever quip. Not a single insult. No challenges to his scientific views. She hadn't even called him by his last name. But then, she hadn't referred to him as Hersch since that morning in the bathroom. She hadn't used "Nolan" much yet, either, but had stuck to "you."

They passed a space where a downed tree had created a hole in the canopy, allowing the sunlight to spill in. Here, some underbrush had managed to grow, and redwood seedlings stretched upward, competing for the opportunity to replace the old giant that had fallen. His dark-adapted eyes drank in all the colors in their most saturated form. In a word, it was magical. Not something you merely walked by as though you found such beauty every day.

He caught her hand. "Let's sit for a while."

She looked down at his fingers curled around hers but didn't pull away. "Tired?"

"I'd just like to enjoy the view." Of course, that had more than one meaning. He'd meant to look at the sunlight, but he wouldn't mind staring at her for a while, too. Odd, he'd fucked her like a maniac, but he hadn't romanced her in any way.

"Okay." She gave him something that resembled a shy smile. He'd seen her grin, laugh, and guffaw more than once. He'd never seen anything like this expression. It warmed a place in his heart he didn't normally pay much attention to, most especially since the day Annie had declared him miserable husband material and had left.

They walked the two steps to the log together as if they'd been choreographed. That shouldn't seem odd, given that their bodies had done a lot of moving together lately. Maybe it didn't feel so much odd as nice.

When they sat, she reclaimed her hand and wrapped her arms around one knee and raised her foot to rest against the log. "Sometimes, I think I'm running a scam on my funding agencies to get them to send me here."

"Hotel Rustic, complete with the world's smallest bathroom," he said. "The very latest in luxury resorts."

"You were the one who wanted to look at the view." She gestured to the clearing where sunlight slanted in, scattering dust motes and small insects around in aimless circles. "You don't find that at the hip beach destinations."

"No, you don't. I know exactly what you mean. I send in a bunch of paperwork for grant proposals—"

"Huge piles of obnoxious paperwork," she said.

"Huge and obnoxious, for sure, but when they stamp 'approved,' I get to go off and follow my curiosity wherever it leads," he said. "That's true luxury."

"It's not as if we get rich doing it."

"Not in money. But after this morning, I don't think I mind cramped showers, either."

She gazed intently into the clearing. Yes, it was beautiful, but her concentration said more about avoiding his gaze than looking at the forest. Still, he could study her with impunity. If she was trying to pretend she wasn't paying attention to him, she couldn't claim he was being rude by staring.

She'd tied her dark curls at the nape of her neck with what women called a scrunchie. As rebellious as the woman herself, her hair refused to be confined, and a few strands had come free and curled around her face. He ought to convince her to share his bed every night so he could see that face when he woke up in the morning.

"Can I ask you something?" she said softly.

"Sure."

"It's personal," she said. "Really personal."

"You can ask. If I don't want to answer, I won't."

"Were you always faithful to your wife?" she asked.

"What?" There went the mood. Of all the insulting things she could have suggested, that one was off the scale. "I cannot believe you just asked me that."

"You said I could ask. If you don't want to tell me, don't," she said.

"But I do want to answer. Of course I was faithful to her. Now, I'll ask you one . . . how the fuck could you think I wasn't?"

"No need to get huffy about it."

"I disagree. I think there are damned good reasons to get huffy." *Huffy* didn't even do the job. *Furious* fit better, as did *irate*. *Umbrage* was old-fashioned and stuffy, but he'd take that, too. In the end, though, he came down to *disappointed*. How could she think that about him?

Could she honestly believe that he was insensitive enough—so wrapped up in himself—that he'd do something that hurtful to someone he'd loved? She couldn't judge his personal ethics based on what he said in his papers and talks. All that was theoretical. Cheating on your wife was personal in about the most destructive way possible. He and Annie had remained friends because they honestly liked each other as much as they always had. But then, maybe they'd liked each other more than loved each other the whole time they'd been together. Maybe he was only now learning about love. The next time he saw his ex he ought to apologize for having been exactly what she'd accused him of . . . a bozo of a husband.

"No," he said. "I never cheated on my wife."

"I'm sorry," she said. "I just kind of assumed."

"From what evidence?"

"Well, the things you write in your papers. The issues we've fought about for years."

"What does that have to do with anything?" he demanded.

She looked at him as if that was about the dumbest thing she'd ever heard. She held up her fingers to make air quotes. "The male's best adaptive strategy is to impregnate as many females as possible."

"That's totally unrelated to how *I* behave."

"Are you or are you not a male?"

She could ask that after the way they'd spent half of their waking hours since arriving here? Okay, probably not half. They had gotten some work done, they'd eaten, washed dishes, and all that other stuff. In fact, they'd had a pleasant walk here and conversation until a minute ago. But they'd spent a whole lot of time doing things that proved his sex and hers. He'd performed at a level he'd never imagined, even during his twenties, when testosterone ran like an IV in his blood.

"Yes, I'm a male, as you may have noticed," he said. "But you also know I study animals, not humans."

"But you don't restrict your discussions to nonhumans. Your research is impeccable, your data convincing. It's when you get to the conclusions part of your talks that the women in the audience start to fidget in their seats."

"They do?"

She actually put her face in her palm. "Honestly, Hersch."

"Nolan."

"When you act that dense, you're Hersch," she said.

Did women have that reaction? He'd always concentrated on this particular woman when she was in the audience. His other female colleagues could be dancing in their chairs, for all he'd notice. He had had some heated discussions with other women in his department. A couple of graduate students had engaged in some loud debate with him in one particular seminar. He'd always enjoyed the spirited give-and-take. He'd never considered that they might actually be pissed off.

Or—oh shit—that those two had felt comfortable confronting him only because they'd provided backup for each other. No single woman student had ever dared. They must have assumed he'd meant his research as a guide to human behavior but had been afraid to speak up. He'd been steamrolling his female students without knowing it. What a prick he'd been.

"I never argued about humans in my papers," he said. "I always made it clear I was talking about elk."

"But some of the others have. Remember the Dalton book?"

How could he forget it? Howard Dalton had relied on a lot of his own work and mentioned him in the acknowledgements. But Howard had taken things farther than Nolan would have, discussing societies where men owned multiple wives and laws that prosecuted female infidelity but not male. That particular book had made it into the general media and created a furor.

"I did not write that," he said.

"Did you refute it?"

He searched his brain for something that would change him from goat to hero in this scenario. Nothing presented itself. "Guilty."

"Look, you're not a bad guy, Hersch."

"Thanks." He heaved a sigh he had no right heaving, given that she was right in everything she'd said about him.

"Nolan," she corrected and placed her hand over his. "I think you understand better now."

"I do. And I'll fix whatever I can when we get back."

"I'm really glad we got to spend this time together." She reached up and took his chin in her hand to turn his face to hers. It was the sort of gesture a man usually did with a woman. He gave in to it, anyway. She'd restored his status as hero, and now, he could lean across the small distance that separated them and kiss her.

Then she leaned back so that she could place her palm against his chest. "You know what?"

He knew he wanted to kiss her, and he knew where that would lead. But given that he finally had her smiling at him, he could postpone the inevitable for a few seconds to see what would come out of her mouth next.

"What?" he said.

"I think you might just win our challenge."

"Not with you having all those extra orgasms."

She bit her lip for a moment. "I like them."

"I do, too. I wouldn't take a single one back even if it meant I'd win," he said.

"Maybe the fact that you can make me climax so easily

means *you're* the champion, not me," she said. "Maybe in our species, giving really is better than receiving."

There. She'd done it again. She'd blown another hole in how he saw the world. When you came right down to it, he'd probably understood sex less than he'd understood love. Sure, he could *do* it well enough, but the moment his mind moved away from the reality of the act, he started spouting nonsense again. DNA receptacles, indeed. What asshole had ever said something so stupid? He probably owed Annie an apology for not getting what the marital act really was about, too, even though he'd given her plenty of orgasms in their married life.

"Interesting concept. You could be right," he said. "Say, did we ever specify a prize?"

She quirked an eyebrow. "Bragging rights?"

"No way. What we do here is private." Contained in this space and time. When they finished here, they'd go back to their respective universities and schedules that would exhaust even the busiest executive. Everything they'd shared would become sweet memories. If you could call anything they'd done with each other's bodies "sweet."

He leaned forward again, inching his mouth toward hers. Still, she held him off.

"You know what else?" she said.

"Is it going to take you a long time to tell me?"

"Sometimes when I'm here all alone and I know there's no one for miles, I . . ."

The blush that suddenly covered her cheeks said he'd enjoy whatever she was about to reveal. "Come on. You can tell Uncle Nolan."

"Uncle?" She giggled.

"Okay, not uncle. Horny next-door neighbor. Spit it out."

"I sometimes take off all my clothes in the middle of the woods, just so I can feel the air against my skin."

Oh, yeah, baby. "You wouldn't happen to feel like doing that now, would you?"

"Only if you would, too."

"Hot damn." He started in on his clothes, but getting them off took some doing because he couldn't take his eyes off Gayle as she stripped. By now, he'd seen her enough that he ought to be able to continue breathing as she revealed herself to him. But no, he had to drag oxygen into his lungs as he gazed at the gentle swell of her breasts, her narrow waist, the flare of her hips. So by the time she'd gotten naked and had even put her shoes back on, he'd only managed to remove his shirt.

She stood before him, mischief in her eyes, as his rod turned to steel in his pants. She was the perfect woman, from the top of her head to the tips of her toes, and especially at the delightful space between her legs. Only one thing could make the view better.

"Go stand in the sunlight," he said.

She cocked her head but didn't move.

"Humor me," he said. "Please."

She turned and walked to the clearing, and now he had a view of the two most beautifully rounded buttocks in the world. They sloped down from her waist and then tucked under. Who would have guessed that a world-class scientist would have a world-class ass like that?

When she stepped into the clearing, sunlight spilled all over her, creating highlights of flame in her hair. She turned slowly to give him a complete view of the goddess she was. Long limbs, alabaster skin, and the easy power of a woman who knew how to celebrate her sexuality.

As he rose and approached, she cupped her breasts in her hands, squeezing and holding them out to offer them to him. He stopped right at the boundary between dark and light, struck still where he was in worship of her.

"Oh . . . my . . . God," he whispered.

She giggled again, and before he could guess what she was doing, she ran away from him, across the clearing, and disappeared into the dimness on the other side.

Running with a crowbar in his pants wasn't easy, but she didn't go at top speed, and he could keep up with an easy lope. In fact, she didn't seem interested in getting away from him so much as she wanted to lead him on a chase. Mostly, she ducked around trees, leaving the sound of her footfalls as directions on how to follow, and she giggled, too. More like a forest sprite than the distinguished professor she'd become once they left this magical setting.

He let her get away a couple of times so she could enjoy herself and so he could let the anticipation build. They were going to make love in these woods, if not this very minute, then soon. He'd get to hear the sounds of her orgasm floating up into the trees. With any luck, she'd scream loudly enough to scare a few birds.

A bit farther off the path, he lost her. They'd entered a stand of truly huge trees, probably first growth and some possibly over a thousand years old. Some of the most magnificent living things on Earth. They might have watched a millennium of mating seasons. The elk, of course, and bears, maybe cougars. He couldn't shake the hope that he and Gayle would be the first humans to couple here.

First he had to find her. He walked slowly among the trees, making as little sound as possible. Hardly daring to breathe.

The clue came as he walked by one of the giants. A sigh so soft he might have thought it was the breeze if he wasn't so attuned to everything about this human female, his mate. As he continued around the massive trunk, more laughter came to him. It had an odd, contained sound, as if it was echoing off something. Or inside something.

The explanation became clear as he rounded one more curve. The tree was hollow at the base, likely the result of a fire that had burned inside it decades if not centuries before. That happened fairly often with redwoods, and they went right on growing. Gayle had "hidden" in there and told him with her laughter how to find him. When he stepped into the threshold, he had her "trapped."

"I thought you wanted to make love outdoors," he said.

"This is outdoors," she said. "Sort of."

She was still completely, gloriously naked, of course. She'd even removed her shoes and set them aside. Keeping his gazed fixed on her in case she decided to bolt again, he knelt to remove his own footwear. She stayed exactly where she was, watching him the way the female elk watched her bull approach.

After straightening, he unzipped his jeans and stripped out of them and his boxers. When she saw the state of his member, she licked her lips as if she'd like to eat him. He might have needed that help right after screwing her in the shower. Maybe. He sure didn't need it now.

"What are you going to do with that thing?" she said.

"I thought I'd let you ride it."

A shiver went through her, strong enough to make her breasts shimmy. "It's very big."

He wrapped his fist around his shaft and pumped. "You shouldn't say things to inflate my ego."

"Even if they're true?" She walked to him, curled her arms around his neck, and tipped her head back to kiss him. The minute their mouths touched, sparks went off inside his body. He pulled her against him, and in a moment they were tangled together so intimately, the boundary between his flesh and hers disappeared. He cupped the buttocks he'd admired in the sunlight, pressing her against his aching cock. The ache turned to a throb as her skin rubbed against the shaft and her belly made contact with the head.

As their lips battled for dominance, seeking more and deeper contact, her hands roved over his back. She dug the tips of her fingers into the muscles there and flattened her breasts against him, making her hard nipples graze his chest. And still, no matter how close they got, it wasn't enough.

Lowering himself to the ground, he brought her down with him. Once he had her on her back, he took his time to explore her the way he should have from the first.

There was a place behind her ear where a nibble of his teeth earned him a purr. She loved kisses along her neck, which she told him by gripping his head as he covered the expanse of skin. His own special treat was the hollow above her collarbone. He dipped his tongue in it and tasted the tang of her exertion. Beneath him, her body writhed. He could plunge his cock inside her and find her ready for him, but why rush things if he could drive her insane first?

Sucking her nipple into his mouth didn't take any creativity, but he stroked her ribs as he did it, urging her upward to meet his caress. By now, the sound of her breathing filled the space around them. If the lover who gave the most won, he'd make sure to be the winner. So when he moved to the other breast and she arched her back, calling out his name, he didn't do the easy thing. He didn't take his place between her legs and drive himself home. He continued teasing the peak with his tongue as he reached to her knee, dipped his fingers beneath it, and stroked the tender flesh there.

She jerked in response, tensing all over. "Damn, what made you do that?"

"Lots of nerve endings here," he answered.

"What are you, an anatomist all of a sudden?"

"Just an expert in sexual behavior."

"I'll say." She groaned and sank back against the floor of their enclosure.

If that could make her groan, she had other places that could create an even more interesting reaction. He rolled onto his side and propped his head on his hand so that he could watch her as he trailed his fingers along the inside of her thigh toward her sex. She had to have guessed his destination because she closed her eyes and let her legs fall apart to invite him to touch her. He didn't rush that, either, but stroked the impossibly soft skin as her breathing became fast and shallow. Inside the walls of the tree, he didn't have enough light to see her chest turn rosy as her arousal heightened, but he'd be able to feel her nectar as it spilled against his hand.

There. He found her clitoris easily, as it had already hardened. When he brushed it with his fingertip, she released a soft cry. Such an amazing organ, the little bud of nerve endings existed only for pleasure—hers to experience, and his to give. His body had nothing devoted solely to sensuality like this miracle, but he could lie beside her and watch her face as she approached the peak and flew over it.

She reached down and placed a hand over his, asking for more, and of course, he gave her what she needed. He pressed her rhythmically, pausing every once in a while to roll her nub between his thumb and forefinger. And every time he did, her breath hitched a little higher.

He knew her well enough to recognize that she'd climax soon, and he took a second to slip a finger inside her. Her sex answered with a release of moisture, the reward he'd hoped for. In a few minutes, he'd feel her wet heat around his cock. She'd take the ride he'd offered, and he'd come inside her with a reaction so powerful only this woman and this place could explain it. But first . . . oh yes, first . . .

When he stroked her clitoris again, her face registered pleasure so intense it looked like pain. "Don't stop. Please, don't stop."

"Never." He continued, now harder and faster. Just what she needed to drive her past the edge. Her voice rose in pitch as her body tensed. He could feel her orgasm in his balls, sense the rush of it through her. And then, she was shouting, her head thrown back, as her hips jerked. Inside her, the walls of her sex would be squeezing and relaxing as the climax continued. He kept rubbing, making the joy of it last for as long as he could.

After moments that hung suspended in time, she went limp, and he removed his hand from between her legs. He gazed at her face as her features relaxed into an expression of pure bliss. His chest filled with wonder.

"Wow," she whispered without opening her eyes.

He leaned over and kissed her forehead. "You're quite a gift, lady."

She rolled onto her side, snuggling against his chest. Her hand snaked over his abdomen and then curled around his cock. "This is the gift."

"We'd better be careful, or we'll end up liking each other."

She finally opened her eyes and gave him a lazy grin. "I wouldn't go that far."

"Okay, enjoying."

"That I can believe. I plan on enjoying you right now."

"So soon?" he asked.

"Insatiable, remember?"

"Right. I'm at your mercy."

"I wouldn't count on any mercy," she said. "I'm going to ride you hard."

"Knock yourself out." He positioned himself on his back and grasped his member by the base. The poor guy had been hard for so long, he needed some relief. She'd give it to him soon. She'd take him inside her and own him the way women had possessed men since the beginning of the species. The next time she climaxed, she'd take him with her. How could he ever have written that claptrap about women not being as sexual as men?

When she swung a leg over him and guided her pussy to take the head of his cock, his mind slid away from work and papers and even the reality of the forest and how he'd gotten to this perfect moment. Nothing in the world mattered except for the way she lowered herself onto him and how he could watch his sex disappear into hers. The wetness he'd felt earlier surrounded him, so hot and wicked. He could so easily forget everything but his own need and rush to the conclusion, but he couldn't leave her achy and wanting. Not his Gayle.

Before he could process that last thought, she began to move in a rocking motion, much as if she were riding a horse. Her inner muscles gripped him on each pass, creating the tension in his sac that would finally finish him. With so little control over his own body, he thrust up into her in time with her movements. Perfectly matched, stroke for stroke, until his heart thundered and blood rushed in his ears.

"How is it you always make me feel this way?" she said.

"What way is that?"

"Oh, God . . . as if I'm going to burst out of my skin."

"You are," he said. "And I will, too."

"I don't want it to end."

"We can always make more."

"Yes." The word came out of her throat like a cry, and she increased her pace, moving, pulling at him, her pussy sucking on him. He kept right on—push, push, push—as if he could penetrate her to her core.

"So good." She gasped. "So good."

He couldn't take any more. He was going to come. No amount of self-control, no high-minded wish to put off his orgasm for her pleasure could stop him. What he could do was make her climax first. She was already so close.

He placed his thumb between her pussy lips, just in front of where he continued to plunge into her. Her clit was hard, whether again or still didn't matter. He worked it for all he was worth, rolling it and pressing it upward. She shuddered and held herself above him as he slammed up into her. Damn it. She had to come now.

As the climax roiled inside him, demanding release, she let out a shout. The walls of her pussy clamped down on him, snapping the last thread of his sanity. As her convulsions began, he emptied himself into her in waves.

They came hard together and didn't stop until light exploded on the backs of his eyelids. And still, she clutched at him, although the spasms became softer and she lowered herself against his chest.

They'd both finished. The climax had lasted only a few seconds but held eternity in it. He managed to wrap an arm around her as they floated in a sea of spent passion. If he'd thought he'd understood sex before, he'd been a fool. The same had to be true of her, whether she'd admit it or not. No one made love like that and came out untouched on the other side.

Chapter Five

GAYLE SMILED INWARDLY as she allowed Nolan to hold her hand while they walked beneath the redwoods on their way back to the cabin. They'd reached an understanding sitting on that log, and they'd forged an emotional connection inside the hollow of the tree. The bond was more than sexual now, more than the sum of the orgasms they'd shared, despite how out-of-this-world those had felt. Anything stronger than an understanding and appreciation of each other would have to develop over time if something were to develop at all. They'd set foot on that emotional path, though, with its frightening power to cause pain or great joy.

As they followed the path, the simple weaving together of fingers carried more emotional weight than fucking, but then, so did curling her body against his after one orgasm and then allowing him to cradle her after another one. With this man, there was no rolling off and saying thanks. The aftermath of their lovemaking had its own significance that mere casual encounters couldn't. The sex act had a new definition for her now, and she'd certainly never look at a hollow redwood the same way.

They didn't speak as they went on. They didn't have to. Body posture, a glance, a smile communicated without words. She'd had sex with him to make a point. Now they'd made love, really made love, and her heart lay in the balance. She honestly cared for Nolan Hersch. Where in hell had that come from?

And what was she going to do about it? She hadn't worried about snickering or rumors because no one was supposed to know what they'd been doing out here in the woods. She'd expected that he'd go back to taunting her publicly, and she'd respond the way she always had, with logic of her own and a heap of scorn for his inability to see the obvious in his own data. Now instead, she'd end up gazing at him like a lovesick undergraduate with a crush on the handsome prof. No that could not happen.

As they neared the cabin, he suddenly pulled her aside and back against a tree. Before she could ask what he thought he was doing, he wrapped an arm around her and pressed a finger to her lips.

"Listen," he whispered.

She did, not hearing anything for a few seconds before she detected the sound of a motor. "One of our vehicles?"

He turned to peer around the trunk. In an instant, he was back. "Susan and Dave. The road must have opened."

Well, shit. Her heart sank as a blanket of disappointment settled over her. No fair. They'd known their time together would end, but did it have to be so soon? Surely, the repair crew had had better things to do than work overtime to end this beautiful fantasy so quickly. She and Nolan had only just connected on a personal level, and they'd hardly scratched the surface of where their sexual life could go.

"Well, lover, this is it. The moment of truth," he said. He gave her a half-assed smile that didn't get all the way to his eyes, but the tension in his jaw said more than his lame attempt at cheer. This turn of events had made him miserable. She probably looked more or less the same.

"Great. What do we do, just walk into camp as if we've been out for a stroll?"

"Can you think of anything else?" He let out a frustrated huff. "I can't."

Any number of things came to mind, none of them remotely possible. They couldn't change sleeping arrangements unless Dave and Susan had suddenly discovered they had an undying passion for each other. They couldn't run off into the forest for quickies during the day and risk having one of the others catch them in some sexual act with each other. They sure as hell couldn't share the shower any longer.

"I guess not," she said. Damn it, this wasn't supposed to hurt so much. She wasn't supposed to care about this man. She'd planned on letting him know in no uncertain terms that she'd won the challenge and that she'd sit in the back of his presentations with a knowing look in her eye. Then, she'd shame him into the truth if he tried spreading any more of his bullshit. Now she knew the person inside his skin and how he could make her spirit soar with his lovemaking. How was she supposed to sit across a table sharing dinner without climbing into his lap for dessert?

The engine sounds got closer and closer and then ended. Voices followed.

"Where do you think they are?" A woman. Susan.

"They must be observing the elk," Dave answered. "They said there'd be a key hidden under the steps. Here."

The cabin door opened and closed and then opened and closed a few more times as the graduate students hauled their gear and supplies inside. Finally, silence returned to the forest.

"Do you think they'll notice we've been rolling around in a hollow tree?" she asked.

"Not unless we take off our shirts."

"We're safe then," she said.

He gave her a rueful smile. "I was planning to scrub your back."

"I was planning a lot more than that." She hadn't figured out the details, but now that didn't matter. She couldn't have him any way at all with the others here. After the research project finished, they'd go back to their respective universities. They'd see each other . . . when? Would things even be the same between them after so much time apart?

"Gayle, I . . ." He heaved a sigh.

"I know. For a while I thought we were getting close to something."

"We were. Something unique and beautiful." He took

her face between his hands and let his gaze bore into hers. "This really sucks."

"It surely does." She wrapped her arms around his ribs and felt the brush of his fingers against her cheek as he tucked her head under his chin. They stayed that way for long minutes as the breeze ruffled her hair and the birds continued calling.

Finally, he tipped her head up and took her lips in a kiss so full of sweetness and promises it made her heart ache. The promises had nowhere to go now. The real world had settled back into place.

After a while, she pulled her mouth from his and rested her cheek against the side of his face. When she felt as if she could breathe on her own again, she straightened and dropped her arms to her sides.

He pushed away from her, holding her upper arms in his hands. "Ready?"

"As I'll ever be."

FAR WORSE THAN she could have imagined, sharing the same space with Nolan Hersch without being able to touch him or even gaze at him was pure torture. Now that she'd decided she not only craved him with every breath but that she actually liked him and enjoyed his company, he had to go ahead and take things a step further by revealing how he interacted with his students. He might have invented the word *mentor*, and it quickly became clear both of them adored him, even Susan. They hung on his every word and basked in his smiles, smiles he gave generously. At the same time, he challenged them and urged them to do the same with him. She was witnessing a master class in the art of teaching, and she'd take some of the lessons back to her department when she left.

When she couldn't tolerate one more moment of his perfection, she retreated to the kitchenette with a stack of dishes. The aroma of barbecue—smoke and the tangy sauce Dave had mixed up—still hung in the air and clung to the plates. They'd had a fabulous meal, and now Nolan had powered up his laptop to illustrate their discussion of the elk they'd be studying.

"This one's Old Bob," he said as she turned her back to the other three and turned on the hot water.

"He's something," Susan replied.

Just a few days before she'd sat in the blind with Nolan as he'd taped the animals. She'd thought him crude and sexist. Hell, maybe he had been. They'd both changed since then.

"How old is he?" Dave asked.

"Gayle would know," Nolan said.

She had to face them to answer. Anything else would be rude. "I've been following him for five years. He's probably seven or more."

Nolan's gaze met hers and held. For a moment, just a moment, she allowed herself to take in the strong line of his jaw and the light of intelligence in his blue eyes. She would not look at his lips. She wouldn't.

He glanced away first, but a hint of color appeared on his cheeks. She felt her own face grow warm. This was unbelievably awkward, but with any luck the others wouldn't pick up on the tension between them. Taking a steadying breath, she went back to work and finally got around to adding some dishwashing liquid.

"Now watch the female," Nolan said. "What's her name again, Gayle?"

"Hattie," she said without removing her gaze from the sink.

"Right, Hattie. See how she's standing her ground. She's inviting her mate," Nolan told the others. The sound of Bob's bugling followed.

"Magnificent," Susan said. "Will we get to see that?"

"Probably," Nolan said. "You two can share the blind tomorrow."

Oh, no. This was not happening. If Susan and Dave took the blind tomorrow for some observation, that would leave Nolan and her alone together somewhere. More incredible sex and then having to face the other two at the end of the day again. They'd have to pretend all over again that they weren't fucking each other's brains out at the smallest opportunity. They were scheduled to be here for weeks. She'd be a basket case after a few days.

"Can I help?" Dave said.

Gayle nearly jumped a foot. Somehow, he'd come right up next to her without her knowing. "I beg your pardon?"

"I can dry or wash," he said. He was a tall, good-looking guy with an easy smile. Early twenties. She'd been that young once and so eager and thrilled to be pursuing a graduate education.

"You just arrived," she said. "Enjoy yourself."

"It's great to be here. I'm excited to have the opportunity to work with you."

"You're Dave Harris, right? You did that journal article with Nolan last year."

"He made me first author," Dave said. "I collected the data, but the ideas were all his."

It had been a solid paper in a good journal. None of Nolan's usual flair for overreach from data to conclusions. He'd given Dave a good start on a research career with the first authorship.

"Susan has an article coming out with him in the fall," Dave said. "He's been great for both of us."

Just then, laughter broke out from the other side of the room. Two voices, one male and one female.

"Who are you, and what have you done with the real Professor Hersch?" Susan said. "You want to study the females?"

"Of course," Nolan said. "The cows decide ultimately which of the bulls get lucky. Bob's good, but even he can't hit a moving target."

Her own words. Gayle clutched the glass she'd been washing so hard she might have broken it if she didn't force her fingers to relax.

"What did you do to him, Gayle?" Susan asked.

"Nothing," she managed to get out, staring into the dishwater.

"Well, something sure changed him," Susan said.

"Let me ask you something. Did I ever . . ." Nolan's voice trailed off for a moment. ". . . bulldoze you with my ideas?"

"You tried a couple of times," Susan said. "I have three brothers. I don't bulldoze easily."

"Thanks for being honest," Nolan said softly.

"You're welcome," Susan said. "But I'm not writing an article with that title."

"Why not?" he said. "At the end of this project, I want you to write a paper on the cow's part in mating behavior."

"But that title?" Susan laughed some more. " 'Getting her to hold still'? Come on, Nolan."

"If the cow doesn't want to mate, the bull gets nowhere," Nolan said. "With Gayle's contribution, we'll document that."

"I am not standing up at conferences to present a paper titled 'Getting her to hold still.' "

"Okay, I'll make the presentation," Nolan said. "It'll be sensational."

"It'll have my name on it," Susan said. "Make him see reason, Gayle."

"Who, me?" She turned to find Nolan staring at her openly. For a few seconds, the gleam of sexual hunger flashed in his eyes. It absolutely stole her breath, sucking every bit of oxygen out of her lungs. Her heart beat like a drum, so loud the others might have heard it. When he looked away, her knees threatened to buckle.

"Dave, maybe I will take you up on that offer of help," she said. "I have a headache, and I think I'll go to bed."

Nolan shot out of his chair. "Are you okay?"

She held out her arms to ward him off. "Fine. I just need to lie down."

Before any of them could express concern or any other damned thing, she set the dishcloth on the counter and went into the room she'd be sharing with Susan for the rest of this trip.

GAYLE WOKE AT dawn, slipped into her robe, and went into the kitchenette to start a pot of coffee. The fog had settled low that morning, swirling among the trees and clinging to the ground. When she approached the window to gaze out at what resembled a world full of ghosts, she discovered some very human, very real activity. Nolan was outside, loading his gear into the SUV. What the hell?

After pulling her robe tighter around her, she let herself out of the cabin and closed the door behind her. He glanced up at her as she approached and then went back to stowing boxes.

"You're leaving?" she said.

He straightened and ran his fingers through his already rumpled sandy hair. "Yeah."

"You weren't going to say good-bye?"

"I'm a coward," he answered. "I left a note in an envelope under your laptop."

"What about Dave and Susan?"

"I left them a note, too."

"Hersch, what is wrong with you?"

"I can't do this." He squeezed his eyes shut and pressed his thumb and forefinger to the bridge of his nose. "I can't stay here and keep my hands off you. It's killing me."

"I know what you mean."

"Last night was hell. It turns out Dave snores. Every time he woke me up, I had to lie there and think of you in the next room. Just a few yards away, and I couldn't be with you."

"Oh, Nolan." She placed her hand against his chest to feel his solid warmth. "What are we going to do?"

"We're going to find a solution, a way to be together."

"How?" she asked. "Our jobs are in different states."

"Your university will have an opening, or mine will. If not, we'll find a third place where they need two people."

She could only stare at the crazy man. "You know how scarce academic jobs are. The chances that we'll find something good are just about nil."

"Then, we'll make better chances."

"How could I have forgotten how stubborn you can be?" she said.

"We're at the top of our field, Gayle. Any department would consider themselves lucky to have us."

"Maybe . . ."

He took her upper arms in his hands as if he could shake his crazy dreams into her. "We'll look for a good faculty opening. We'll both apply. Whoever wins will negotiate a research job for the other."

"You can't give up teaching, as good as you are at it," she said. "That'd be a crime."

"Stop putting up obstacles." He nearly shouted that last. If he wasn't careful, he'd wake the others. Then he did something even more stupid. He pulled her against his chest and kissed her, and the feel of his mouth on hers was good enough to evaporate reality. She answered as if an eternity had passed since their lips had last met. He'd addicted her to the taste of his mouth, and now she couldn't get enough.

Too soon, he pushed her away. Both of them were breathing hard, as if they'd just run a mile. If alone, they would have been pulling off each other's clothes already.

"All right," he said, his voice unsteady. "I'll start the search as soon as I get back."

"What do we do in the meantime? Do I sneak into your hotel room at conferences and tie you to the bed?"

His blue eyes sparkled. "Sure. Why not?"

"Be serious."

"I am serious . . . about both of your suggestions," he said. "I've never been tied to a bed."

He was right, at least about sneaking into hotel rooms. There really wasn't any reason anyone needed to know who was sleeping in what bed at a conference. Tying him to a bed held quite a bit of appeal, too. But would that make the foundation for a real relationship? "I guess we could do that."

"We'll find other opportunities to be together," he said. "Whatever it is we've created together, I'm not giving it up. I'm not giving you up."

"All right." She threw up her hands in surrender. "You've convinced me."

He let out a long breath, as if he'd been holding it inside, waiting for her answer. Did the foolish man actually think she could turn him down? Pulling off his ideas would take luck and a whole lot of work, plus some serious negotiating skills. They'd manage because they had to. They'd crossed over a border at some point since arriving here, very likely inside the hollow trunk of a redwood. Neither of them could go back. They could only go forward.

"You stay here with the students," he said. "Make sure they get some good data we can use for a joint paper."

" 'Getting her to hold still'?"

"It has a certain ring, don't you think?"

"It certainly sounds like one of Nolan Hersch's sensational creations," she said.

"Ours, not mine."

"You're right about that, too." With the fog hushing everything around them, she snuggled into his arms and bathed herself in his warmth. Everything would turn out as he'd dreamed because it had to. He'd make sure of it.

"And in the meantime, why don't we come back here . . . alone?" he said. "After all, mating season isn't over yet."

Liked *Mating Season*?
Be sure to read all the novellas
in Alice Gaines's
Cabin Fever series

Heat Rises

Storm Bound

and

Brief Encounter, an erotic short

Keep reading for an excerpt from

Heat Rises

Chapter One

SO MUCH FOR making it to her job interview. Laura Barber might as well have been looking at a moonscape rather than a deserted mountain highway. Still shivering, she gazed out the window of the country store as the falling snow covered the pavement and filled in the road completely. The storm had started only half an hour ago. What would this place look like by morning?

"You're a mighty lucky young lady," said the shopkeeper, handing her a Styrofoam cup with steam coming out the top. "If you'd gone off the road any farther from here, you'd still be out in that."

She took a sip of the coffee and did her best not to grimace at the bitter taste. The man may be right about her luck, but she'd probably ruined her shoes on the trek here. The low-heeled pumps had cost a bundle, and she'd worn them just enough that her feet felt comfortable when she dressed for business.

"Yep," the man said as he gazed out at the accumulating snow. "Nobody'll be moving around in these parts for days."

"Mister—"

"Beaumont," he said, offering his gnarled hand.

"Mr. Beaumont," she said, studying him as they shook hands. The twinkle in his blue eyes suggested more youth than the fringe of white hair did. If you called central casting for a country store owner, they'd probably send someone like this man.

"You'd be in a heap of trouble if you'd broken down farther away," he said.

"Can someone come out and put me back on the road before things get worse?" she asked.

"You don't understand storms in these mountains, Miss."

"Ms.," she said. "Ms. Laura Barber."

"Well, Ms. Barber, won't nobody get out of here until the plows come through."

"When will that be?"

"Days," he answered. "Probably not a week, though."

"A week?" Darn it all. She was supposed to be at the bottom of this mountain by evening and at an interview in the morning. She'd planned carefully to get ahead of this storm, but her plane had landed late. Still, she ought to have been able to make her destination. She'd grown up in Connecticut and had driven in winter weather before. Snow was snow, wasn't it? Apparently not.

"What am I going to do?" she asked. "I can't stay here for days."

"That you can't. I'll be closing up and heading home in a few minutes."

"Is there a motel nearby?" she asked.

"Nope. We'll have to find a family to put you up."

"I can't impose on strangers for days."

He shrugged. "Don't see that you have much choice."

Wonderful. Not only would she not make it to her interview but she'd also have to spend days with people she didn't know. She managed well enough in business situations where procedures and rules of engagement were clearly laid out. In someone's home, she'd have to interact. She probably couldn't disappear behind her laptop without appearing rude.

"Unless . . ." Mr. Beaumont said. "Your solution might be pulling up right now."

Headlights shone in from outside—bright enough to blind her for a moment—a huge SUV or pickup, with its engine at a low roar. The motor shut off, and the lights went dim. A man climbed out and headed into the store. A blast of cold air whooshed in through the front as he entered. "Hey, Phil."

Mr. Beaumont shuffled off. "Hey, you young pup. What are you doing out in weather like this?"

"Business down in the city. Thought I could outrun the storm."

The voice tugged at her memory. Low and dark. She knew it. Even though she hadn't heard it recently enough to place it in her brain, something about the tone registered in her body.

She glanced over at the counter where he stood, his

back was to her. Tall and broad-shouldered, he commanded the space around him. She had a physical memory of that too, enough to warm her skin. Whoever this was, she'd do best to avoid him. But how?

"Good thing you're here," Mr. Beaumont said, gesturing toward her. "This lady is going to need a ride somewhere."

The man turned, and all the memory nudges turned into one huge sucker punch. Ethan Gould.

Good Lord, not him. It had to be five years . . . no, six. That night at the party. After three years of fantasies about the handsome guy who always sat at the front of the class, she'd decided to at least try to find out if the attraction was mutual. Tequila fortification, too much, had led to a night of humiliation. Oh God, all the things she'd said to him. A queasy feeling settled into her stomach remembering them after all this time.

Other than that, they'd almost never spoken to each other all through business school. He'd have forgotten her by now. Women probably came onto him all the time—women more remarkable than her. He wouldn't remember. Please God, don't let him remember.

Sure enough, he smiled at her as he would at any stranger. A genial expression he used so easily. The famed Gould charm would come next. So potent, it even worked on men. On women . . . well, forget trying to resist it.

After a moment, his brows knitted together. "Do we know each other?"

"No . . . I don't think . . . haven't met," she said. Damn it all, how could he force this reaction from her after so much time? She'd actually lie about her identity if she could get away with it. She'd avoided him successfully since that horrible night. She'd actually followed his career so that she'd know where he was. He couldn't have just happened on her on a snowy mountain, and yet, here he stood, as tempting and as terrifying as he'd been at that party.

"This is Ms. Laura Barber," Mr. Beaumont said. "You two know each other?"

"Right." Recognition dawned in his amber eyes, followed by a slight tension to his jaw. Remembering, no doubt. Her skin went from warm to burning. By now, her face would be a bright pink.

He recovered quickly, with a big smile. He still had perfect teeth, of course, and perfect skin. Only his too-large-ish ears kept him from total perfection, but the flaw made him all the more attractive.

"It's been a while," he said. "Good to see you again."

"Hi." A stupid reply but innocent enough.

"Seeing as you two know each other, won't you mind taking Ms. Barber to where she wants to go?" Mr. Beaumont asked.

He rested a hand on a nearby rack of magazines and struck a casual pose. A light of cunning in his eyes belied his apparent ease. "Where are you headed?"

"The city," she said. "I'm already late."

"How'd you get this far?"

"Rental car"—she gestured toward the outside as if she could point at the thing—"I ran off the road."

"Can't say I'm surprised," he said, his gaze never left

her face. She did her best to look straight back at him, but she'd never win a staring contest with this man. Eventually, she gave up and studied his shoes, instead. Boots, rather—the sort ranchers wore. His had a broken-in appearance, as did the faded jeans that covered his legs up to the hem of his shearling jacket.

"We won't be getting to the city tonight," he said. "But we can make it to my friend's cabin."

"Cabin?" she repeated. "In the middle of a blizzard?"

"My friend's an engineer. The place is self-sufficient with a generator and solar panels."

"The sun's not out now," she said. In fact, with the heavy snow, it was already dark.

"And storage batteries," he said. "We'll be fine."

"I haven't agreed to go with you."

"What choice do you have?" he asked, as he straightened and pulled a slip of paper from his jacket. "I'll need a few things, Phil."

"Coming right up." Mr. Beaumont took the list from him and retreated to the back of the store.

"Look, this is really nice of you—"

Before she could get the "but" out, he took a step toward her. " 'Nice' isn't exactly the word I was thinking of."

She made herself stand her ground, even though everything in her wanted to back away. "I don't want to impose."

"Don't be silly. No one around here would put someone out on a night like this."

"Mr. Beaumont said he'd find a family here to take me in."

He crossed his arms over his chest. "So, you're a social butterfly now? Happy to move in with strangers for several days?"

Damn him, he knew she wasn't. He had to remember from graduate school that she kept to herself, quietly getting top grades from her place in the back of the class.

"I . . . I . . ." Damn it. He actually had her stuttering. She took a breath. "I can't go with you."

"Why not?" he asked, as he studied her, his gaze assessing and not without a light of admiration. Her heartbeat responded, speeding up. The feeling might be pleasant with another man—one who hadn't heard about her sexual fantasies after she'd had too many margaritas. She'd told him about how her mind had wandered during boring lectures, imagining how his hands would feel on her breasts. About how she played images of him in her mind when she used her vibrator. She'd even asked if his sex was as big as she'd imagined it, and then giggled when she'd fumbled against his pants and discovered it was even larger. Oh God, humiliation. Utter and total humiliation.

"Maybe you're afraid to be alone with me," he said. He might have read her mind.

"Ridiculous." Okay, that was a lie, but she wouldn't cower before him. She'd gone on from that night to establish a good career. As a grown woman with more experience since graduate school, she shouldn't have to fear men any longer, even this one. Even if she did, she wouldn't let him know he frightened her.

"Laura, you have a choice of crowding in with a family you don't know or sharing a cabin with me. I won't even speak to you if you don't want."

"I don't think that will be necessary." Great. She'd agreed to go with him. No matter. A few days together, and she'd get away again.

"Good." He smiled yet again, the blasted man. "The cabin it is."

You COULD HAVE knocked Ethan Gould over with a feather. First, to run into Laura Barber at Phil Beaumont's store, way out here in the middle of no place. At least, there was a logical explanation for that. She was probably up for the same job at Henderson that he was. A bit odd, that, as their talents—skill sets, she would have called them—lay in very different areas. But they were both übercompetent, as any headhunter would have to know. Still, what were the chances that she'd end up at that country store, needing a ride in one of the mountains' worst storms of the season just as he pulled in? Fate was trying to tell them something, and he, for one, was listening.

The fact that she'd end up staying with him in an isolated cabin fell into a different category of unlikelihood. Impossibility, more like. And yet, there she sat in the bucket seat next to his, staring out at the snow as if it held some message.

Laura Barber, the shy thing who'd turned into a wild

woman one night, nearly dragging him into an empty bedroom at the end-of-semester party. The woman who'd promised sex so uninhibitedly; she'd singed the edges of his imagination. The woman who never spoke up in class but who'd whispered filthy words in his ear while she'd unfastened his belt and started in on the zipper of his slacks. Unfortunately, she'd given off enough clues of her intoxicated state to keep him from following through, just barely managing to stop things before they'd gone too far.

Laura Barber . . . the one who got away. Hell, the one he'd let get away. Damn his conscience all to hell.

"Do you own this truck?" she asked after several minutes of silence.

"Rented."

"Do you always drive something so big?"

Right. The queen of green. "What were you driving?"

"A hybrid."

"If you'd had one of these, you wouldn't have gone off the road."

"Touché." She looked him in the eyes for probably the first time since she'd climbed aboard. "Truce?"

"Sure." Although, how he'd manage that would take some mental gymnastics. She wore the same scent she had all through business school. Nothing exotic, just kind of clean and sweet. She'd wrapped the scent around him that night. It still went straight to his gut, and now, he had the mother of all hard-ons. Truce, indeed.

He stared out the windshield. "That your hybrid up ahead?"

She squinted, peering forward. "It is."

He pulled up beside the car, set the brake, and pushed the gear lever to park. "Leave the engine running for heat. Give me your keys."

"I can get my bag myself."

He held out his hand. "I thought we had a truce."

After fishing in her purse, she produced a key on rental company chain and handed it over. Now, he could get away from her perfume for a few seconds. Maybe the cold would do something to ease his boner too.

He climbed out of the truck and shut the door behind him. His boots sinking into snow halfway to his knees, he trudged the few feet to the hybrid and used the key to open the trunk. She traveled light—just one carry-on and a suit bag. If he looked inside, which he wouldn't, he'd no doubt find a formless skirt and jacket combination. She could almost, but not quite, hide her plush figure under all the layers of clothing she wore.

After closing the trunk, he scrambled back to the truck and stowed her things in the back. Then, he took his seat in front and set the gear to low to take them down the snow-covered highway.

"You seem to know your way around," she said.

"I grew up near here."

"You look the part. All you need is a Stetson." She actually smiled. Not much but enough to curve that tempting lower lip. No matter how hard she tried to blend into the woodwork, that mouth and her enormous brown eyes kept her from pulling it off. Great, now he was thinking about her mouth.

"What are you doing in these parts?" he asked, even though he had a pretty good idea of the answer.

"Job interview," she answered.

"Henderson?"

"How did you know?"

"My interview is day after tomorrow," he said. "Doesn't look as if either of us is going to make it."

She groaned. "Oh no."

"Don't worry. You still have a chance."

"Why wouldn't I?" she said. "They'll understand about the storm."

"I didn't mean that. I meant the competition."

"What . . . oh." She glared at him. "You don't think I can beat you for the job."

He didn't answer but only smiled.

"Competitive to the end, eh?" she said.

"Pot . . . kettle."

"Is this your idea of a truce?"

"Sorry. Force of habit." He turned the truck off the main highway onto the narrow road that led to Jeff's cabin. Here, even the four-wheel drive wouldn't help them if he made a bad move. He'd have to concentrate on something besides the chaos in his jeans. The heavy vehicle inched along while the wipers slap-slapped against the windshield and the wind howled outside, swirling the snow around them. Laura sat huddled in the corner, her arms wrapped around her ribs.

"Frightened?" he asked.

She bit her lower lip. Even a short glimpse of that out

of the corner of his eye put his mind in places where it didn't belong.

"A little," she said after a moment.

"I'll take care of you." Boy, howdy, would he. *Stop it, damn it. Now.*

Normally, she'd have bristled at any suggestion that she needed help with anything. She must have been really scared not to say a word but just sit there, making herself small. If he weren't careful, she'd start tugging at his protective instincts. But then, when had he ever been careful where a woman was concerned? Well, maybe once . . . with this woman.

"Is it much farther?" she asked.

"A few more yards." Of course, in a storm in the mountains, a few more yards could stretch on forever. How had the pioneers ever managed?

The cabin came up on him unexpectedly. He must have misjudged how far they'd come because the outline of the building appeared directly ahead of them before he'd realized they'd arrived. He let a breath out slowly, and his shoulders relaxed. Though he'd never admit it to Laura, navigating under these conditions was a bit of a crapshoot, and he hadn't felt all that comfortable himself.

He steered the truck into the carport and cut the engine. When he turned off the headlights, they fell into darkness for a moment. All the better for him to sense the woman next to him. Her scent and the sound of her breathing filled the space around him. It was going to be an interesting few days.

IF THE CABIN had appeared rustic from the outside, the interior somehow managed romantic and high-tech at the same time. Laura left her ruined shoes in the enclosed entryway, what Ethan referred to as a "mini mudroom," and followed him into the main living area. When he hit the switch, lights came on around the baseboards, producing enough illumination to suggest the interior of an elegant restaurant.

"Solar power?" she asked as she tipped up her carry-on and draped the suit bag over it.

"From batteries beneath the house," he said. "The system gives off heat as well as light."

"And the heat rises to fill the room."

"Once I get the woodstove and a fire going, we'll be toasty."

"Nice." They'd been bandying that word around a lot. This time, it didn't carry extra meaning.

Ethan put the bag of groceries on the counter in the kitchenette. "Settle in."

She glanced around. "Are there other rooms?"

"Bathroom."

"Then, where would you like me to settle in?"

He paused in the act of stowing a carton of eggs in the refrigerator. After a moment, he straightened, placed his elbow on the door and assumed his too-casual pose again. "You take the sleeping loft. I'll camp out on the couch."

She checked the piece of furniture in question. "Is it big enough for you?"

"I'll fold into it."

"Because, I don't really have to—"

"Take the loft. As you observed, heat rises. You'll be comfortable up there."

The baseboard heating was having an effect on the temperature, but not enough for her to remove her coat.

"I'll lay a fire," she said.

"You know how to do that?"

"It's not rocket science."

"Be my guest."

While he continued putting away groceries, she went to the huge stone fireplace and knelt to check out the supplies. Plenty of wood and kindling. Starting with crumpled newspaper, she built what should soon be a good blaze. She found matches, lit the paper, and sat back on her heels to watch the fuel catch.

Out of nowhere, a male hand appeared in front of her, holding a glass of red wine. She took it and glanced up at the towering figure of Ethan Gould. "Thanks."

"I didn't know for sure if you'd want anything to drink."

"I'm good with wine. It's tequila I need to stay away from." Damn it, why had she said that? She shouldn't have mentioned anything that could remind him of that night. Or remind herself, for that matter. She sipped some of her drink and stared into the fire.

Of course, he didn't do the easy thing and go back to the kitchenette and leave her alone with the memory. Oh no, he had to sit down beside her in front of the fire.

"Want to talk about the two-ton elephant in the room?" he asked.

"No."

"I do."

"Fine," she said. "You talk. I'll listen."

"Doesn't work that way."

"Look, Ethan." She took a fortifying sip of her wine and let it roll around on her tongue. He had good taste, she'd give him that. Eventually, she had to face him. When she did, she somehow ended up lost in the reflection of the fire in his eyes.

"Laura . . ." he prompted.

"I wasn't myself that night." Lord, how embarrassing. If he wanted to talk about this, why didn't he say something or do something? Why was he putting it all on her? "I behaved inappropriately toward you."

He gave her a lopsided smile. "Is that what they're calling it now?"

"Please. You'll make me blush."

"So what?" he said. "No one's ever died of blushing."

She could. Her heart fluttered in her chest, and her stomach felt full of cold lead. When her hands trembled, she set her glass on the hearth rather than spill red wine on the carpet.

"Hey, hey." He put his glass next to hers and took her hands in his. "It's not that serious."

When she couldn't take any more gazing into his eyes, she switched to staring at the fire. "You could probably have sued me for harassment."

"Harassment?" he repeated. "How do you figure that?"

"You obviously didn't welcome . . . um, return feel the same . . ."

"Because I didn't follow through?"

She clenched her teeth together and sat in utter, silent shame.

"You'd had too much to drink, Laura," he said. "Only a bastard takes advantage like that."

"Well," she pulled her hands from his and took a steadying breath. "It was a long time ago. I'm glad we settled it."

"I don't call that settled," he said.

She stared into the fire again. If she didn't look at him, maybe he'd go away. "I do."

"Damn it, Laura, you're going to deal with this." Taking her chin in his hand, he turned her head until she had to look at him. "Do you know how exciting you were that night?"

"I was drunk and disorderly." Drunk enough for him to have rejected her but not enough for her to have forgotten all the things she'd said to him. No one on earth had ever heard of her fantasies, but after that encounter, this man had.

"You turned me on like crazy," he said. "I went nuts trying to figure out how to get you to make the same invitation sober."

"It was a long time ago, Ethan."

"I would have called you, but I figured that would have embarrassed you."

"I'm glad you didn't."

"I kept putting myself in places where I'd bump into you by accident, but you disappeared"—he gestured with both hands—"poof."

"I don't want to talk about this," she said. "You promised."

He studied her for a long moment before picking up his wine again. "Yeah, I guess I did."

"Thanks for understanding." This time, when she lifted her glass, it didn't wobble.

"You'll at least eat dinner with me, I hope."

"Of course," she said. "This is excellent wine, by the way."

"It should go with the steaks. How do you like yours?"

"Rare."

"Rare it is." With the knuckle of his free hand, he tapped the end of her nose before rising and sauntering back to the stove.

She took a deep breath—the first truly relaxing one she'd had since he strolled into the country store—and watched him rinse vegetables for salad in the sink. She ought to help him, but he seemed to know what he was about. Besides, the world was a safer place with distance between them.

So, he'd refused her that night out of gallantry. Or so he said. That made things marginally less humiliating. Sort of.

As he worked on their dinner, his movement fluid as he went from counter to refrigerator to cabinet and back, she couldn't erase the memory of that lean body against hers. The kisses . . . sweeter and more potent than the margaritas that had caused her to lose control. And the misery, the soul-crushing disappointment, when he'd pushed her away.

Now that they'd discussed the two-ton elephant, the whole incident was closed. Over and dealt with. Finito. Somehow, that made her stomach only queasier.

About the Author

ALICE GAINES loves her romance as hot as she can get it. Besides spinning tales in her head, Alice's passions include vegetable gardening, the San Francisco 49ers, and *America's Test Kitchen*. She's a maniacal fan of East Bay soul band Tower of Power.

Alice has a PhD in psychology from the University of California at Berkeley and lives in Oakland, California, with her pet corn snake, Casper, and a strange cat that moved into her yard.

ABORCA... is her her romance artist as she earns...
it besides sculpture takes in her head, while a passion for
that, was... and, ... this, and features as... as, and
campus... TRIA latest ... also a supplied has the... for her
self-hand power of novel.

... has a child in anthology... how... how... a... of
California ... and her and lives in Oakland, California
with her personal make, Gaston, and a... one of... life...
novel... her own.

Give in to your impulses . . .
Read on for a sneak peek at three brand-new
e-book original tales of romance
from Avon Books.
Available now wherever e-books are sold.

NIGHT OF FIRE
THE ETHER CHRONICLES
By Nico Rosso

STORM BOUND
A CABIN FEVER NOVELLA
By Alice Gaines

THE SHORT AND FASCINATING TALE OF ANGELINA WHITCOMBE
By Sabrina Darby

An Excerpt from

NIGHT OF FIRE
THE ETHER CHRONICLES
by Nico Rosso

Night of fire, night of passion

U.S. Army Upland Ranger Tom Knox always knew going home wouldn't be easy. Three years ago, he skipped town, leaving behind the only woman who ever mattered; now that he's seen the front lines of war, he's ready to do what he must to win her back.

Rosa Campos is long past wasting tears on Tom Knox, and now that she's sheriff of Thornville she has more than enough to do. Especially when a five-story rock-eating mining machine barrels toward the town she's sworn to protect.

Tom's the last person Rosa expects to see riding to her aid on his ether-borne mechanical horse. She may not be ready to forgive, but Rosa can't deny that having him at her side brings back blissful memories . . . even as it reignites a flame more dangerous than the enemy threatening to destroy them both.

CHAPTER ONE

The Sierra Madre Mountains, California

He wore his gun. And hoped he wouldn't have to use it. The war was behind him. Tom Knox headed west.

His saddle creaked. The ends of the leather reins slapped lightly against the body of his steed. The wind whistled in his ears. Six hundred feet below him, small hills gathered into a larger mountain range.

Instead of being filled with screaming ether-charged bullets and explosive cannon shells, the sky here was peaceful. A red-tailed hawk skimmed below him, head twitching from side to side, tracking prey. In the distance, three turkey vultures spun wide circles over a shady hill. Tom was part of the calm. His Sky Charger kept a steady pace, pushed by the high whispering whir of the tetrol-powered fan at the back.

Weeks ago, the skies to the east and behind him had burned. Enemy airships and friendly Sky Trains had blazed brighter than the sun as they crashed toward the vast soya fields of the Great Plains. Men had fought and died.

As an Upland Ranger in the U.S. Army, he'd seen it all. He'd smelled the gunpowder and felt the recoil of his Gatling rifle as he fought to turn the Hapsburgs away from American soil. A couple of searing hot bullets had found their way into his flesh, but he'd healed fast enough to get back onto his ether-borne Sky Charger and fly into war.

Tom leaned forward, patting the cool zinc metal neck of the charger. Strange modern times he was living in. When he'd left this territory three years before, it had been on a real horse.

Adjusting the levers at his stirrups, he took the charger higher into the air. Tall pines whisked beneath him, then thinned as the rocky peaks took over. White patches of snow clung to the shaded angles of the mountains like forgotten sun-bleached bones.

Just at the top of the range, Tom stopped his charger and turned to look behind him. The battlefields and scarred skies were hundreds of miles away. The fighting wasn't over. The war waited.

He stared into the distance, remembering all the Hapsburg soldiers alive and dead who'd aimed their guns at him.

Keep your pants on, he thought. *You'll have plenty of chances to put me in a grave later. Until then, I'm heading home.*

Kicking the charger's levers, he powered the one-man ether airship over the mountain ridge, leaving the flat expanse of the east at his back. The mountains spread out into hills that bunched and gathered like an unmade bed. The winter's green still lasted, revealing the fertile farms and orchards that took advantage of any flat land.

Tom squinted behind his goggles and pulled the brim of his black cavalry hat low. The far horizon was a bright silver knife's edge. The Pacific Ocean. He could already smell the salt, even this far inland. A few more miles and he'd hear the gulping squawk of the seagulls that rode the high wind currents. It felt like home.

The hairs at the back of his neck stood up, same as if he and other Upland Rangers were flying out for a dawn raid on a Hapsburg artillery camp. There were plenty of dangers at the front lines of the war. And battles to be fought at the home front.

The Sky Charger picked up speed. Tom felt himself pulled into the inevitable.

He reined back on the mechanical steed and wound over the hills. Twisted oaks dotted the land. Through the lenses of his goggles, they almost looked like their branches were outstretched arms, warning him. But there was no turning back.

The war had stopped to take a breath. Tom and the other front line soldiers were allowed some time of their own. Without a fight in front of him, his compass spun. There was no answer other than west. Home to Thornville.

And Rosa.

A needling voice in his head sounded a lot like his younger self, mean with an edge of whiskey on its breath. *Surely seeing her again will go as smooth as silk*, it mocked him.

He tugged at the knot of the black bandana around his neck. The charger dipped closer to the ground, heading toward a shady notch running between the hills. The mechanical flying horse didn't shiver or twitch its muscles in response to coming closer to home.

Tom took a long breath and spoke in a whisper quickly lost to the breeze. "Nothing was ever easy with Rosa."

Don't lie. Looking at Rosa had been easy. Before he'd left town three years ago, he could sit and stare at her until all the candles burned down in his one-room shack. There seemed to be no end to the depths of her large, dark brown eyes. Black hair framed her face, high cheekbones, and full mouth. Tom had memorized every detail. He didn't need to carry a small lumiscopic picture of his sweetheart like other soldiers did.

But she wasn't his sweetheart anymore. A stolen horse and a moonless ride out of town had made sure of that.

Maybe a raid on a Hapsburg camp would be easier than going home after all.

The sound of the charger's tetrol engine was quickly drowned out by the loud roar of a rushing river. It tumbled along a winding path, and Tom followed it, trading the steady sun for shade. Where the river widened and calmed, he took the charger even lower, toward the water.

If the mechanical horse had had legs, it would've been standing chest deep in the water. Tom tipped his hat back, letting it rest against his shoulders by the stampede strap. He pulled off his goggles and clipped them to the leather lanyard slung over his shoulder. The other end of this lanyard was looped through the butt of the pistol on his hip. He didn't need to look to know it was still there after the long flight over the planes. The weight of the Rattler was a steady presence.

Leaning low over the side of the charger, Tom dipped his bandana into the cool river water. The silk danced in the flow, tugged by the current, pulled toward Thornville and Rosa.

He drew the bandana from the river and used the cool cloth to wipe the dust from his face. After tying it around his neck, he went back to the water, filling his canteen, taking a long drink, and filling the canteen again. Mountain water tasted of cool stone, pure and fresh. A relief after the muddy streams of the Great Plains.

He unbuckled the auxiliary reservoir from one of the saddlebags. The Sky Charger wasn't a real horse, but he still had to water it. He filled the tin tank with water and then screwed on the top.

Everything was squared away. Tom could keep moving. But he stayed, hovering over the running water.

That voice kept stabbing at him. *Rosa's down at the river. Doing the wash, or collecting water. Probably gathering blackberries. Safe and secure, like her parents wanted for her. Not like anything you could've given her. No land, no family. Just a wildcat breaking horses for hourly pay.*

Tom tried to swat the voice away as if it were a night mosquito, but it went on. *Bet she took Parker's offer and married him. That guy was a great carpenter.* The dull brass of the wedding band around Tom's finger seemed almost black in the shadows over the river.

He kicked the Sky Charger's ascend lever and climbed higher into the sky. Parker built nice things. Cabinets and tables and a stable life. His tools had been handed down from his father and his father's father. All Tom had of his family was a dead-end last name and the saddle he sat on.

The voice in his head was silent but present, mocking him. Tom responded to himself: *I'm gonna play it as cool as snowmelt when I see her.*

Horseshit. His younger self spat and took a drink from a cloudy bottle.

Tom countered, *I can be a gentleman and tip my hat and congratulate her on her marriage.*

But when he saw her parents, that would be another story. Tom shifted his weight in the saddle, feeling the Rattler on his hip, the Gatling rifle in the scabbard at his knee and the knife in his boot. Might need every bit of hardware to get out of a "conversation" with Rosa's mother and father.

After the din of the front lines and the skies raining fire around him, all he should have wanted was a little peace and quiet. But if that were true, he'd have found another mountain range or another town, where no one knew his name. He had to go to Thornville. Even if there was no one waiting for him, no yellow ribbons, no family. He'd just drunk his fill of river water, but thinking about Rosa made him thirsty all over again.

"Peace and quiet." He said it out loud as if that could make it real. "How hard can that be to find?"

The river bent and dove into a jumble of rocks. Tom pulled on his hat and flew higher, breaking from the trees and nearly running straight into the side of a five-story mobile mining machine.

He yanked hard on the reins, wheeling in the air to avoid the wooden slats that made up the outer structure. A blast of invisible heat washed over him as he passed an exhaust stack from one of the tetrol engines that powered the lumbering beast. All of the cool calm he'd pulled from the river burned away.

"What in holy hellfire . . . ?"

Turning the charger again, he dove toward one of the men who walked next to the giant machine. Tom had to shout over the sound of the giant conveyor treads that propelled the beast forward.

"You boys got a lot of nerve breaking up the scenery out here."

The man tensed slightly, revealing a black rotary shotgun slung over his shoulder and an ether pistol in a holster. A lot of hardware for a dude in a pinstripe suit. Tom's Rattler was ready at his hip if he needed it.

But, hopefully, words would be enough and he could leave the shooting to the war. "What claim you headed to?"

No response from the man. He only turned and looked at Tom. It was almost like a piece of the mining machine had broken off and started walking like a human being. The man wore a leather and brass mask that encased him from his bowler hat to his jaw. A shiny brass capsule covered the man's mouth, and a flexible metal tube ran from the mask to a cup attached to his ear.

"Goddamn." Tom had seen this technology before on guards stationed around a bank in Chicago. "Whisperers."

The din of the rolling mining machine swallowed the man's low words, but Tom could tell he was saying something by the way he moved. The communication was broadcast out to the others around the device, and they all turned to look at Tom. Sunlight glared off the glass goggles built into the masks. There were at least twenty Whisperers, all armed and coordinated by their masks.

Even though everyone knew there was over a million dollars' worth of gold locked in that Chicago bank, no one dared take on the Whisperers to try and nab it. It was like facing a single man who had forty eyes looking in every direction and guns at the ready.

"I get that you won't tell me your claim, but there's got to be a gang boss around here who can talk."

The men just kept watching him as the machine rolled forward. It was still folded up for travel, but when it reached its destination its teeth would be deployed to eat through anything in its way. Giant saws, grinding wheels, and conveyer belts would stick out of the front, tearing apart a mountainside and drawing it inside the device. Then automated sifting trays would shake the debris, searching for gold or silver or whatever the mining company had decided was valuable that day.

"We all got a job to do." Tom's patience was shrinking, crushed under the treads of the mining machine. "But you're dealing with a sergeant in the U.S. Army Upland Rangers. I'm asking you a question, and you're obliged to answer me."

The man moved and Tom nearly drew his Rattler. The first bullet would hit the Whisperer in the chest, if things came to that. But Tom's reflexes were good enough to hold off on shooting the man. The pinstriped man wasn't going for his gun; he was merely pointing at a spot on the mining machine.

A brass plaque riveted to the side of the rolling monster read: MODEL IV. CRANDALL MINING COMPANY. SAN BERNARDINO, CALIFORNIA.

"All right then, it's someone else's problem." He kicked a

lever on his charger, rising higher in the air. "Just wish your machine was as quiet as you dudes."

The technological din was left behind. Tom was back in the quiet and calm of the sky. *That's right,* he told himself. *Let everyone else deal with the world's problems.* He'd been fighting fiercely for months, and it felt like the United States had been holding its breath while trying to resist the Hapsburg advance. Now was the time for a sigh of relief. Some brave sons of bitches had snuck deep into the enemy's homeland and blown up a key munitions plant.

Those shock waves carried all the way to the Great Plains. One minute Tom was running belt after belt of ammo through his shoulder Gatling rifle, trying to pick off flying skiffs full of Hapsburg shock troops; the next minute the bad guys were circling their airships way behind their lines and trying to figure out what to do next.

"I know what I'm doing next." He licked his lips as the landscape rolled far below him. Saying it out loud might make it real. "Chicken. Berry pie. A shade tree . . ." That was how he and Rosa would spend long summer days at a hidden spot at the bank of the river. Her kisses were always sweeter than any berry they found in the brambles.

Goddamn, it might have been the worst idea to come back. He didn't want to see her. A new life, married and happy and safe and secure with someone else. He had to see her, even if she hated him. There was only one bit of pleasure he'd known in this world, and it was Rosa. The rest was hardship. His thirst returned. But being close to Rosa again without having her might be like drinking fire.

Tom had never seen this country from these heights. This was the territory he'd grown up in, but the land seemed so different. He experienced it like a dream, knowing it was right but feeling something was wrong. He was lost but knew where he was headed.

Keeping the distant shining ocean to his left, Tom rode north. The river flickered below him, a snake hidden in shadows. He crested a hill, then another. Homesteads appeared in the flats. And in a far clearing at the base of a tall mountain he saw Thornville.

Three years had pushed the town farther into where the trees had stood. What had been one wide road was now two, a cross of buildings with boardwalks and even a clock tower. Houses were scattered around the town. There was more to this area than just farming and canning blackberries now. Maybe one of those houses was Rosa's.

His mouth went dry. She was close. There were people out on the street, but he couldn't identify them or know what they were up to from this distance. Could she see him high in the air?

Tom had left Thornville by riding away on the dusty trails. He returned in the air, a different man. But would Rosa know that?

He'd snuck out of town on a stolen horse. Coming back straight down the main street wouldn't be right. Tom curled a wide arc around the approaching town, putting the silver sea to his back. The pines and scrub oaks were still thick enough on the other side of the river to give him a nice private place to land.

He brought the charger down, leaves brushing against

his thighs, and took the metal head right next to a thick tree. While the hovering craft was still four feet off the ground, he dismounted. The ground under his feet didn't feel stable after all that time in the saddle. He took a few steps to loosen up, then pulled on the side lever of the charger, bringing it to the ground.

"Rest easy, girl. You deserve it." He locked the Gatling rifle in its scabbard, then lifted the metal covering at the charger's flank, exposing some of the inner workings. One flip of a switch and the tetrol engine stopped chugging. Tom reached deeper inside the body, to where the ether tanks glowed green through their glass ends. "Wish I could give you an apple." Instead he yanked on the pins next to the ether tanks' valves and slipped them into his shirt pocket.

The tanks stopped catalyzing ether, and the charger rested completely on the dirt. Tom gave it one last pat on the side. Dry oak leaves crunched under his boots as he walked toward town. The smell of their dust took him back to being a boy, running through this land, trying to find tarantulas or deer bones. Not long after that, he'd been sneaking around these parts, searching for Rosa.

Tom pulled a plump blackberry from a thicket next to the river. It was sweet and reminded him only of her. The plant's thorns barely scratched his toughened skin. Could he avoid Rosa's thorns?

The old bridge—with some new wood—still spanned the narrow part of the river near town. Here it was, the last place he'd seen her. The running water tumbling over the rocks sounded like the echoes of him and Parker yelling at each other. Couldn't have been the way Parker wanted his marriage proposal to Rosa to play out. The carpenter might've been expecting some tears of joy, certainly not her storming off while Tom and Parker bloodied their knuckles on each other. But Tom had been freshly burned by her parents and didn't take kindly to another man moving in so fast and asking for his girl's hand. And taking on Parker was a fight he knew he could win.

Tom shook off the memories and stepped closer to the river. As he crossed the bridge and got closer to town, he realized that the echoes weren't the lingering ghosts of his final clash with Parker and Rosa. The yelling was real. There was trouble in Thornville.

He picked up his pace, following the sounds of the conflict. Someone was getting punched and going down in a lot of pain. Others shouted encouragement. Tom certainly didn't want in on a brawl, but even if everyone in town had forgotten his name, Thornville was still his home.

Ducking between a candy shop and a women's dress store, Tom got his first look at the main street. Six or seven men stood in a wide ring around two fighters. One of them staggered on wobbly legs, trying to make fists. The other stood his ground, ready. Something flashed on his chest, making Tom blink away the bright streak across his vision. A tin star.

"Aw, hell," Tom muttered. "Just the sheriff running some drunks out of town."

The badge flashed again, and Tom refocused his eyes on the sheriff.

It was Rosa.

An Excerpt from

STORM BOUND
A CABIN FEVER NOVELLA
by Alice Gaines

In the latest installment in Alice Gaines's steamy Cabin Fever series, one woman throws caution to the hurricane winds and explores her deepest sexual fantasies when a storm leaves her stranded on a tropical island with two hot studs.

AN AVON RED NOVEL

CHAPTER ONE

When the time came, Christie had to use every ounce of willpower to make her feet take her to the dock. As she descended the steps that led to the ocean, she passed the plantings the gardeners had so carefully arranged to look haphazard, wondering how roughly Fred would treat them. Most weren't native to the island but had been chosen for their ability to thrive in ocean breezes, and sunlight filtered through the palms overhead. The tiny pink orchid flowers had just begun to open. Would they be here when she came back?

It was stupid, really, to worry about things here. The whole sales pitch about safety and security had facts to back it up. Still, she'd so much rather stay and see for herself. Tomorrow she could check on things if she remained. More important, she could explore her sexual opportunities with Wolf and Jon if they remained with her.

When she arrived at the beach, she stepped onto the dock and walked to the end where the ferry would stop. Sighing, she set her few bags down and waited for her "rescue." The ferry wasn't far away, and now it puttered closer and closer.

She really ought to go back up and collect her guests. Though the first clouds hadn't appeared yet, the storm was bearing down on them. They didn't have much time to get to the airport and get a flight out.

Captain Joe stood at the helm of the small vessel. When he got to the dock, he tossed her a line, which she tied around a piling. With no more than a dozen seats on benches, the boat hardly qualified as a ferry. No one occupied them now. He'd come for only Jon Carlson, Wolf Martin, and her.

Captain Joe smiled at her and then glanced behind her. "Where are the rest of the passengers?"

"At the hotel. Finishing packing." That wasn't true. They'd probably finished long ago. She just hadn't told them the ferry had arrived. Why did this have to be so damned hard?

"They'd best hurry. I have to get my boat back and stowed before the storm hits."

"Uh, yeah," she said.

"Christie? Is everything okay?"

Christie could not make herself answer. The memories crashed through her mind, tumbling over each other. Her first glimpse of the two businessmen, dressed in suits as if they had to impress her. They hadn't needed to dress formally to do that, but the elegant cut of their clothing had emphasized their lofty positions on the corporate food chain. An easy exercise of power, a pure aphrodisiac. Then, they'd turned into beach bums, endearingly boyish.

Oh hell, all that was nice, but the sizzling glances sealed the deal. Jon's easy, knowing smiles. Wolf's suggestion that they open personal negotiations. Every cell in her body knew by instinct that she could have one or both of them. Every primitive part of her brain promised to punish her for months, if not years, with fantasies of what could have been if she let them go now. Only the tiny part of her mind called "rational" or "conscience" told her to let them go. The "want" and "must have" parts could squash rationality and doing the right thing like a bug. In fact, they did.

Squish. Dead.

She might as well face facts. She wasn't letting Jon and Wolf off this island until she'd explored every inch of their bodies or died trying.

"Christie?" Captain Joe rubbed his chin in puzzlement. "Talk to me."

"Right." She smiled, returning his gaze as innocently as possible. "What I meant to say is I'm sorry you came all the way out here for no reason."

"I always come out here at this time of day."

"Of course, but you must have preparations to make before the storm closes in."

He continued to study her as if she wasn't making any sense. Maybe she wasn't, but one way or another, she had to get him to turn his ferry around and leave before one of the men realized their escape from getting trapped here had arrived.

"There's still some time to get back to the mainland ahead of the storm," the captain said. "But I don't know when I'll get back out here."

"Good, you go on. The two executives have sent for their own boat," she said.

"They have a boat?"

"Their company does. You know how these business types are. They like their luxury."

"You're sure?" Captain Joe rubbed the back of his neck. "I didn't see anyone."

"Absolutely sure. It should be here in half an hour or so."

"What about you?" he asked.

"I'll go with them. We'll be fine. All three of us." That had all come out too high-pitched and too fast. She didn't lie often enough to get good at it.

"Okay then. I'll shove off." He didn't move for a moment, though, but kept studying her. She gave him what ought to look like an innocent smile—she didn't normally practice those, either—and met his gaze head-on, even though her heart was pounding in her chest. If they stood here much longer, either Wolf or Jon was bound to appear. Not only would she have to say good-bye to them, but Captain Joe would no doubt ask them about their company's boat.

"You take care," Captain Joe said after what seemed like ten minutes but could hardly have been more than a few seconds.

"Oh, I will." She'd take care of herself by taking care of the two men—first one, then the other. She bent to untie the line from around the piling and tossed it to Captain Joe so he could cast off. When he opened the throttle and directed the ferry away from the shore, she waved to him. Finally, he and his craft became no more than a speck on the horizon, and she turned to go up the path to the hotel, taking her first deep breath since he'd arrived. She left her bags to collect later and headed back to the hotel.

Neither her guests nor their luggage had made any appearance, so they wouldn't have seen the ferry either arrive or leave unless they'd been watching from the terrace, and she'd seen no evidence of that. Now she only had to concoct some story for why the three of them had been stranded. An emergency on another island ought to work. Someone who'd had to be hurried to medical care. She'd think of something before she had to confront them.

Instead of worrying about that, she let the fantasies run free while she climbed the steps again, walking beneath the palm trees toward the huge windows overlooking the terrace and the sea. Reinforced shatterproof glass, they should weather a gale bigger than Fred would create. They'd get quite a view of turbulence outside while they enjoyed themselves inside.

Wolf and Jon. Which one should she have first? The tall blond with the easy smile, or the smaller, more intense man with the fierce blue gaze?

Oh sweet Lord. She stopped in her tracks for a moment. Or ... she could have them both together. Two such competitive males. Could she get them to work together to give her sex more erotic than she'd ever hoped for? A threesome, her very own. She could have them both at once ... a cock inside her while she sucked on another one. When one man tired, the other could take over. They could go on for hours that way.

But why stop there? Oh my. Once all inhibitions had dropped, they could experiment with anything that came to mind. They could role-play—say, horny wife with the next-door neighbor when her husband comes home unexpectedly.

Or better—she could let them dominate her. She'd admired their easy sense of power from the first moment she'd set eyes on them. She could experience that directly. Total surrender to their sexual needs and her own. Just imagining it made her knees weak. Oh my God, could she really have that?

Not only could she have any sexual fantasy that occurred to them, but she could have them completely to herself with no one looking on and judging. No gossips. No stories to get out. She could indulge herself in every way possible. The only limits she'd have to face would be Jon's and Wolf's reservations, if they had any.

She was risking a lot. A hell of a lot. Losing their business, for one thing, if they found out she'd lied. And if they were angry enough to tell the company why they'd bailed on Santa Inez, there went her job, too. Perhaps the worst would come if she had to face their anger and disappointment. That didn't make much sense, given that she'd met them only the day before. But she'd enjoyed Jon's easy smiles and Wolf's approval of everything she'd shown him at the resort. Seeing all that evaporate because of her dishonesty would hurt. She could end up miserable and unemployed, all because she couldn't control her hormones.

She couldn't change that now. All she could do was hope for the best and enjoy herself. Perhaps if she did a really good job of making them happy, they'd forgive her if they did find out.

Damn it all, what was wrong with her? The only way they could learn of her deception was to talk to Captain Joe, and they had no way of doing that. She picked up her pace until she fairly skipped up the last few steps.

When she arrived inside the hotel, they were both waiting for her, luggage on the floor between them. Neither beach bums nor captains of industry now, they wore casual clothes—lightweight shirts and slacks. No matter how they dressed, they were mighty fine to look at. Now maybe she'd have the chance to feel Jon's long arms around her and burrow into the firm planes of Wolf's chest.

Jon bent to grab the handle of his suitcase. "Ferry waiting?"

"Uh, no." *Think, think.* She needed a story when all her current thoughts came through X-rated. "There was an emergency on another island. High-risk pregnancy. She had to get to the mainland in case she needed a hospital in the next couple of days."

The two men exchanged glances.

"You mean the ferry left without us?" Jon asked.

"It never came," she answered. "I got a message on my cell phone."

"We're stranded?" Wolf asked.

"I'm afraid so," she said. "There's no time to get another boat out here in front of the storm."

"And none likely to come soon after the storm, either," Wolf said.

"I'm sorry."

Neither of them gave much of a clue as to how they felt about being stuck here. They couldn't be happy about missing their business engagements or they would have volunteered to stay. They didn't convey any skepticism about her story, either. But neither of them was dancing with joy, either.

"Look at it this way . . . I'll get to show you that the resort can weather even a mild hurricane," she said. "I think you'll be impressed."

"What about electricity?" Wolf asked.

"We have a generator and solar power," she said. "We were getting ready to open, so there's plenty of food and a well-stocked bar and wine cabinets."

"And a restaurant kitchen to play around in." Jon finally gave a clue to some emotion as the light of competitive mischief entered his eyes. "My partner here claims he knows how to use a chef's knife. What do you bet he's blowing smoke?"

Wolf heaved a sigh. "You never give it a rest, do you?"

Christie almost matched his sigh with one of her own, out of relief. If they were upset with her, they weren't showing it.

"We'll see who can really cook," Wolf said.

"That we will," Jon answered. That might be innocent enough except for the way they were both staring at her. With any luck, they'd all three be cooking by that evening.

"Do you buy her story?"

Jon pulled his head from the restaurant freezer long enough to glance at his friend and partner. Wolf stood on the other side of the butcher-block worktable, an open beer in his hand.

"Ms. Lovejoy's?" he said.

"She's the only 'her' around here," Wolf answered.

"What makes you think she lied?"

Wolf lifted one shoulder in a shrug. "It just seemed strange. One minute, we were all ready to go. The next, there was a mysterious cell phone message."

Jon thought back. He'd been too busy concentrating on how the top of her sundress stretched over her breasts to notice much of anything else. But she might have avoided their eye contact. Bad liars did that. Wolf had a great sense for people. He might be on to something.

"Do you really care if she's telling the truth?" Jon asked.

"Don't you?"

"I guess." Although he hadn't managed to push his fantasies of Ms. Christie Lovejoy naked completely to the back of his mind, the state-of-the-art professional kitchen made for a pleasant diversion from the constant state of semi-arousal he'd endured since noticing how she moved—as if she were dancing with a man who really turned her on. Gleaming stainless steel appliances, more sauté pans than he could ever hope to dirty, and a six-burner gas stove with enough BTUs to fire up hell itself. All that could entertain him until he could watch her face when he first sank his cock into her.

"We're getting a free vacation in a gorgeous location," he said. "Don't overanalyze it."

Wolf took a drink of his beer while he considered that. "It's a matter of principle. Deception like that rubs me the wrong way."

Jon studied Wolf for a minute. "Why are you twisting yourself into knots about this? We won't even be dealing with her after we leave here."

"I like my lovers to be honest with me."

Jon laughed. "Dream on, pal. She's mine."

Wolf's eyes widened. "You want to make a bet on that?"

"Why not? Although I hate having to beat you."

"You won't. I'll fuck her first," Wolf said.

"I wouldn't be so sure of that, if I were you."

"Well, what do you know? We're competing for a woman," Wolf said. "We've never done that before."

"First time for everything." Jon studied the contents of the freezer again. On one shelf, he found packages labeled "pork ribs," and on another, individually wrapped game hens. On the last he hit pay dirt. A box that read "Strip Steaks, USDA Prime." He pulled it out and set it on the worktable. "I give you our dinner."

"Anyone can cook a good piece of beef," Wolf said.

"I'm talking steak Diane," he said. "I'll feed her dinner and then eat her pussy for dessert."

"Have you told her that?"

"Not in so many words." He opened the box to find steaks sealed in airtight plastic pouches. Beautifully marbled, they were not only prime but really first class. He removed three and returned the rest to the freezer.

"Have you said anything to her on the subject at all?" Wolf asked from behind him.

Jon shut the door and leaned against it. "I don't have to talk. Hell, I could tell within a minute of meeting her, she was the type of woman who likes to fuck."

"Every woman likes to fuck if her partner takes the time to turn her on."

Jon laughed. "Bragging much?"

"Reality." Wolf drained his beer and set the bottle on the table. "And as much as you like to pretend you're an asshole, deep down you're too nice to be selfish about sex."

"I have a surprise for you, partner. Deep down inside I'm actually a very shallow guy."

Wolf rolled his eyes. "Bullshit."

The man knew Jon too well to fall for his I-don't-give-a-damn persona. They'd shared everything since college, including tips on how to make a woman's body hum like a finely tuned instrument. He couldn't hide the fact that he took pride in satisfying his partners any more than he could deny Wolf did the same.

"You know, we've never had the same taste in women before," he said.

"I like curves," Wolf said. "You like thinner women."

"Not true. I don't care much about body types. I want a woman who isn't afraid to come on strong—one who lets me know from the get-go that she's hot, willing, and available."

Wolf rested his hip against the worktable and remained silent for a moment. "You're right. You always did go for the uninhibited type."

"Women on the plump side tend to be shy about their bodies. It's a crime, if you ask me."

"So, Christie Lovejoy has my perfect body and your perfect personality."

"And you're going to lose her to me," Jon said.

Wolf laughed. Let him. Jon had pegged Christie Lovejoy as his perfect bedmate the moment he'd set eyes on her. Even at their first meeting, when the three of them had kept everything strictly business, she'd walked with a swing of her hips that said "fuck me now." And her mouth . . . watching her eat was an exercise in sexual frustration. She savored everything, taking her food slowly and deliberately. From there, he could so easily imagine her lips around the tip of his cock as she closed her dark eyes with pleasure. He'd hold the sable hair back from her face so he could watch her sucking and licking and . . .

Well, great. He'd given himself a full hard-on just thinking about her. Wolf was probably in the same state. She'd tried to take a good look at both of them and had glanced away, biting her lip, when he caught her at it. Unless he'd misjudged her interest, he'd satisfy her curiosity about his cock soon. Maybe tonight. He needed only to get her alone for a while, and she and his boner would become well acquainted, indeed.

"Say, Jon . . ." Wolf said.

That got his attention. Wolf almost never used his name but usually addressed him as "hey you"—when he wasn't calling him "asshole" or something equally affectionate. "Say, Jon" meant something worth listening to would follow.

"Wolf," he answered.

"Have you ever done anything, um, unusual in bed?"

"You mean, like kink?"

The wheels turned in his partner's head for a moment. "Yeah, that. And maybe . . . sex in groups."

Jon's mind immediately went back to one particular summer when his girlfriend's college roommate missed a plane and ended up spending the night with them. "I almost had a threesome with Roz and Sue."

"Almost?"

"Roz said it was okay, but she gave off some strange vibes. I called it off."

"But never one woman and another man."

"Not so far, but you know my slogan: 'Never say never.' Are you bringing this up for the reason I think you're bringing this up?" He didn't have to say her name. The two of them were trapped on an island with a woman they both wanted.

"Maybe I am," Wolf said.

"Then remember my other slogan: 'If it feels good, do it.'"

"That sounds like you."

Wolf started opening drawers and checking out the contents. Conversation over. The fact that he'd brought it up was revealing enough. His mind was going in new directions, and now Jon's was, too. Fascinating.

"How are you going to handle missing Komura?" Jon asked.

"He won't like it," Wolf said. "He has to have hands-on attention or he feels snubbed."

"You'll have to buy him flowers and kiss and make up."

Wolf stopped in the act of pulling a knife from the block that held it. "How about your contract negotiations?"

"I guess Howard can handle it."

"He won't get a deal as good as you can," Wolf said.

"It's time he learned to try."

Wolf inspected a twelve-inch chef's knife and humphed in admiration. "If Christie Lovejoy is keeping us here under false pretenses, she's showing a bad lack of ethics."

"Or she's showing us that she needs to get laid."

Wolf rolled that around in his mind for a bit. Jon knew what Wolf was like when he sorted things out. He had a good head for business and for life in general.

"While I sympathize, I don't approve," Wolf said finally.

"It's not only dishonest as far as business is concerned. Keeping us here for sex is personal, too."

"Up close and personal," Jon said. "Just the way I like it."

"Don't you take anything seriously?"

"Orgasms," he answered. "I take orgasms very seriously."

"So you're going to sleep with her no matter what."

Jon chuckled. "I don't know about you, partner, but my plans for her don't include a lot of sleep."

"You're incorrigible," Wolf said.

"And you're going to turn her down if you don't like her ethics?" Jon asked. "Give me a break."

"No, of course not." Wolf blew out a frustrated breath. "But if I find out she's been lying, I might extract my pound of flesh."

"Well my pound of flesh is hot and hard and ready for some fun."

An Excerpt from

THE SHORT AND FASCINATING TALE OF ANGELINA WHITCOMBE

by Sabrina Darby

WANTED:

A beautiful young woman—preferably one with no connections, who won't ask too many questions—to spend two weeks in the North of England with an obstinate, aloof, and utterly handsome man.

Must love dogs, fixing up crumbling castles, and gorgeous and complicated war heroes who may or may not be hiding hearts of gold under their gruff exteriors.

Must not, under any circumstances, fall in love . . .

Simpering misses need not apply.

Chapter One

March 1816

Dear Cousin,

I still despair of ever seeing my Georgie matched.
There is one thing unchanged about my son, and that is
that nothing his mother says can make him see reason.
As a result, I've taken your advice and have placed an
advertisement in the paper. I can hear you now in my mind,
claiming that you were teasing and never intended me to
realize such an action. However, I am at my wits' end and
thus have undertaken a diabolical scheme. As I am not
entirely certain my son is comfortable with ladies, I thought
perhaps to test the waters, so to speak, by finding him a
mistress.

Yours,
Mary

The last time Angelina Whitcombe had been this far north, it had been the end of summer, when the loveliness of the rolling green earth of the Dales was at its finest and the river sparkled in the sunlight.

Now, it was spring, and snow still clung stubbornly to shady corners, and mist lingered over the faded road dotted with rocks and fallen trees. Thankfully, she'd prepared for every eventuality of weather. After all, everything she owned was packed into the trunk, back at the inn. It had been a bit of a shock to see twenty-two years of life fold down into a space four feet by two feet.

Through the canopy of branches she glimpsed a sight of grey. The tower. Finally.

And it wasn't all that far away.

She picked her way around yet another large fallen tree branch. The winds had ravaged the area, and no one cared enough about this overgrown road to clear it. But once upon a time, people must have traversed it daily, otherwise no one would have thought this area important enough to build a castle.

To build the now-ruined tower house in which Mrs. Martin claimed her scarred and diffident war hero son had hidden himself away. It seemed fitting enough for a gothic novel: ruined castle, ruined man.

With a slight twist, for Angelina's employment was to seduce the poor invalid, reawaken in him a sense of the erotic, and then encourage him to seek a wife. She had little doubt she could do the first. After all, she was no simpering virgin. She'd been the mistress to two well-pleased men. Beyond that, she was an actress born and bred, spawned by a family of actors.

But as for the last . . . well, she'd find a way to fulfill her duty in some fashion. Regardless, she'd walk away from this transaction a hundred pounds richer. Once she would have scoffed at that sum of money, but not now. Her value in London had plummeted, and a hundred pounds could keep a wise woman for years.

She stopped, took a deep, calming breath. There was no point in anger or resentment. She had to focus on the task at hand, which required being charming and frothy, lifting a man out of the depths of despair.

She shifted the leather-bound sketchbook she carried from her left arm to her right, rolled her shoulders back in a stretch, and then started forward again. If this traipsing about country lanes were to become a habit, she would need sturdier shoes.

The lane turned to the left, and suddenly the trees opened into a clearing, and the castle was before her on a slight rise. She frowned.

It wasn't a very large castle. In fact, it was neither picturesquely ruined nor perfectly kept up. It looked . . . disheveled more than anything.

Fitting. She could feel wisps of her hair against her cheeks and neck. Likely she, too, looked a bit disheveled. Preferably, she would look windblown and rosy cheeked, the very picture of bucolic English femininity.

She stopped again halfway up the glacis, catching her breath. When she'd been a young girl, she'd run across hill and dale, skipped across meadows and scampered in rivers.

Now, she was already tired after the long walk from the village, and this small elevation was taxing her greatly.

As she took several deep breaths, she studied the tower. The thick wooden door was ajar. Excellent. It would be much easier to saunter in as if she thought the place abandoned than to have to knock and beg entrance.

She trudged uphill. As she neared the door, a clanging filled the air and the earth seemed to shake. She stopped again and listened carefully, trying to identify the discordant sounds. Mrs. Martin had assured her that Captain H.J.G. Martin, or, *my poor Georgie,* was the only occupant of the castle, but what if he was not here? What if ruffians or highwaymen had taken up residence? What if she was about to put herself in a situation far worse and more dangerous than the one she had left behind in London?

She looked around. She could flee now, head back to the village. Although, really, now that she'd come all this way, it was a bit late for those sorts of thoughts.

Forward again.

The clanging had more of a rhythm now, sounding like metal against wood. Maybe this Captain Martin was not alone but had hired a carpenter or some other craftsman to bring the place to rights.

She slipped through the doorway. Hesitantly, she walked across the dim entryway and entered a large room. The great hall, she imagined it would have been called. Here, light streamed in through windows high off the ground, and straight ahead flames simmered in the large fireplace.

The clanging continued, but there was no one in this sparsely furnished room.

"Hello?" she called out. She slowly crossed the hall, running her hand over the lone table, covered with rolls of paper, that stood in the middle of the room, pausing by neatly folded blankets and a pallet of straw by the fire. She eyed the large wooden tub tucked to the right of the big stone hearth.

Someone lived here. *Slept* here.

Captain Martin or a squatter?

The conditions were worse than the ones she had grown up with as a child in an impoverished traveling theater troupe.

"Is there someone here?" she said, projecting her voice as loudly as she could. It echoed off stone walls. The clanging hesitated, continued for a moment, and then, finally, stopped. She was scared to leave this spacious, empty room, to venture into more shadowy spaces beyond the archway to her left.

Instead, she focused on a stack of books beside the makeshift bed. Curious, she knelt down, feeling the warmth from the fire on her face as she reached for the one on top.

She heard the panting a moment before a large furry animal charged at her.

She swiveled her head, lost her balance, and slipped back onto the floor, her sketchbook falling to the side. The dog, a collie, pressed its large wet nose against the side of her face.

"Jasper, heel. Who the devil are you?"

Wonderful. Likely the dog's owner was Captain Martin, and there was no graceful way to rise from such an indelicate position on her own.

She looked up, raising her arm for assistance, and then dropped her hand.

Her jaw, too, before she caught herself.

He was bare to the chest, and magnificent. Strong, with

muscles as defined as if a sculptor had chiseled them from marble, skin glistening from some recent physical exertion. The clothed parts of him were wonderful too. Her gaze slid down the lines of his hips and thighs, reaching the place where the superfluous fabric of the trousers obscured what were surely equally fine calves. How could they not be? This man in front of her was some god of male perfection.

"Madam." There was a hardened edge to that voice, and, reluctantly, Angelina lifted her gaze to meet his. Which was obdurate, and yet he smirked at her. As if he were both angry and amused.

"I'm very sorry to disturb you," she said at last, lifting her hand towards him for assistance once more. She punctuated her words with the smile that had charmed audiences across England. "I'd been told there was a ruined castle to see. I thought it abandoned until I heard that ruckus. Help me up, will you?"

He stepped forward out of the shadows, and she gasped at the sight of the jagged scar that cut from cheek to chin, twisting his lips up on one side. There wasn't anything amused about this man looming over her. Now she'd made the situation worse by staring.

At least that shocking feature confirmed without a doubt that this man, who looked the antithesis of shy and sickly, was the very man she intended to seduce. The way he fairly radiated masculinity, this wouldn't be hard at all. In fact, it would be her *pleasure*.

"This is a private residence," he said, even as he reached his hand out. His large, strong, bare hand that made her wish she weren't wearing gloves. She placed her fingers on his palm and used her ballet training to rise to her feet as gracefully as possible.

He had a very warm hand.

When she was standing, looking up into that scowling, smirking face, she didn't let go.

"Yes," she purred. "I see. Do you live here . . . alone?"

He snatched his hand away, stepping back. Looked pointedly toward the front door.

Of course, she couldn't leave. And now that she'd seen him, she didn't really want to. What she wanted to do was run her hands over his naked skin, lick the small nipples that dotted the fine smattering of hair across his chest. While sexual relations had mostly been an economic transaction for her, while this would be at the heart of it all, too, she rather thought she'd want to taste this man even if she weren't being paid.

Which was stupid. Was the way women like her went from being beloved mistresses of Marquesses and Earls to roadside whores.

No. She had a job to do.

"I'm in Yorkshire to draw the dales," she said into the charged silence. "I've stopped at The Golden Lion in the village, and they assured me Castle Auldale is as ruined and picturesque as old abandoned castles come. 'Tis a pity I only draw landscapes. You are equally picturesque."

His eyebrows rose, and he crossed his arms, but still he didn't speak. Just watched her with that expression, which was confused by the perpetual twist of his lips.

"What? Surely you have women fainting in your path wherever you go? You cannot be ignorant of your physical appeal?"

His arms fell back to his sides. He looked deliciously nonplussed. Which meant she had the upper hand. Which meant he was just where she needed him. Intrigued.

"Who are you?" he said, the words hissing through the air.

"Angelina Whitcombe, and, as I said, I'm traveling for the scenery."

"Traveling alone?"

A prickle of awareness awakened the skin at the back of her neck.

"Yes, in fact, I am."

His gaze ran down her body, slowly, purposefully, as if he wanted to make certain that she knew exactly what he was looking at.

"A lady never travels alone."

The best lies were half-truths, so she smiled brilliantly at him.

"Darling, I don't have much of a reputation left to lose."

"*I don't have much of a reputation left to lose.*"

He believed her. He just didn't believe that devil-may-care, forward façade. No, there was the hint of something much deeper, and much darker, beneath his intruder's flippant words.

Not that it mattered.

He wanted this Whitcombe woman out of his home, away from the solitude he'd so carefully cultivated. If he'd wanted human company, he would be living in the manor house half a mile across the dale.

"But I do," he said at last, reaching down to pick up her

leather-bound sketchbook. "So I must ask you to leave." He held the book out to her, tempted to open it and see just what she had been sketching during her *tour* of the English countryside. She snatched it away.

"I suppose I should be getting back before it grows dark. I embarked on my walk rather late in the day." But instead of leaving, she swept past him toward the archway that led farther into the keep. "What *are* you doing in here?"

He strode after her, shaking his head. He grabbed her by the elbow before she could leave the room.

She stepped back as if he'd pulled on her harder than he had, and all of a sudden an armful of soft, warm woman pressed against him, blonde hair tickling his nose.

He took a deep breath, which was a mistake. The scent of muguet and spring air infiltrated him, clouded his thoughts.

"You have the advantage of me, sir," she whispered, her voice low, seductive. "If we are to touch so intimately, I should at least know your name."

"John," he choked out, releasing her as if she were a flame. He did *not* wish to be intimate. "John," she repeated. She made his name sound like a word lovers whispered in the dark of night. She turned to face him. "What secrets are you hiding?"

Secrets. He had no secrets. Everything about his life could be found in the local church records, in the army register, in the files of the Board of Ordnance.

He didn't know who this woman was, but he knew she was dangerous. He knew she was taking him away from the work he wanted to do, the work that was helping him, saving him. She was the outside world seeping in.

"Out," he demanded. "Now."

He must have looked frightening. God knew he had scared enough children with this scarred countenance of his. She, too, had gasped when she'd first seen him. Now she winced and retreated.

Good. She should think him dangerous. What woman in her right mind would stand in the middle of a ruined castle talking to a half-clothed stranger? He was a man, stronger than she was. He could rape her, kill her. No one would ever know.

He closed his eyes tight against memories. Against the deafening sound of metal striking metal, wordless battle cries, and explosions. Against the smell of blood and gunpowder.

She was walking away, the soft soles of her shoes tapping against the stone floor. He felt her passage like a sweet spring breeze, the scent of lilies cutting through his mind.

He opened his eyes. Through the speckled, gauzy midafternoon light streaming from the high windows, he caught the last flutter of her blue cloak as she turned the corner, the ribbons of the bonnet in her right hand streaming behind.

Jasper whined.

John looked down. The dog kicked its legs, begging for attention.

"All right, Jasper," he said, bending down to pat the dog's flank firmly. "That was unexpected, but it doesn't change anything. We have work to do and only a few hours of daylight left."

At the moment, work was repairing the kitchens.

Next month, don't miss these exciting new
e-book love stories only from Avon Books!

TURN TO DARKNESS
by Jaime Rush

New dangers expose the ugly past Shea has worked so hard
to bury. Though she feels she doesn't deserve love, she suddenly has three men who want her; one wants to possess her,
one wants to love her, and one wants to kill her. Greer, who
pledges his life to protect hers, has a dangerous secret of his
own—the Darkness that turns him into a territorial panther.

THE FORBIDDEN LADY
by Kerrelyn Sparks

Let the spy games begin! When Quincy Stanton—Loyalist
by day and traitorous spy by night—meets Virginia Munro, a
lovely fellow patriot who's become entangled in her own brand
of spy games, Boston doesn't seem big enough for the two of
them. Forced to join together to fight the British, they'll face
the biggest question of all: what happens when attraction gets
in the way of espionage?